Praise for Melo

Love Gently Falling

"Ms. Carlson pens an uplifting tale of love, family, and courage."
— *RT Book Reviews*

Once Upon a Winter's Heart

"A sweet, quick read that celebrates love's beginnings as well as the spirit of Valentine's Day."
—Serena Chase, USAToday.com

"A delightful story about the loss and recovery of romance, love, and hope.... *Once Upon a Winter's Heart* will revive any-one who's given up on romance and wants a happy ending."
—*Family Fiction*

"Melody delivers all that is sweetest and best about love in this Valentine's novella and does it with a tasty dash of Italian spice. Now that's amore!"
—Robin Jones Gunn, bestselling author of
Sisterchicks in Gondolas

"A sweet love story, *Once Upon a Winter's Heart* is a beautiful picture of the joy of being swept off your feet."
—Melanie Dobson, award-winning author of *Love Finds You in Mackinac Island, Michigan* and *Where the Trail Ends*

Your Heart's Desire

ALSO BY MELODY CARLSON

Love Gently Falling

Once Upon a Winter's Heart

Available from Center Street wherever books are sold.

Your Heart's
Desire

MELODY CARLSON

CENTER STREET

New York Boston Nashville

Center Street
Hachette Book Group
1290 Avenue of the Americas
New York, NY 10104

www.CenterStreet.com

Printed in the United States of America

RRD-C

First edition: January 2016

10 9 8 7 6 5 4 3 2 1

Center Street is a division of Hachette Book Group, Inc.
The Center Street name and logo are trademarks of Hachette Book Group, Inc.

The Hachette Speakers Bureau provides a wide range of authors for speaking events. To find out more, go to www.HachetteSpeakersBureau.com or call (866) 376-6591.

The publisher is not responsible for websites (or their content) that are not owned by the publisher.

Library of Congress Cataloging-in-Publication Data

Carlson, Melody.
Your heart's desire / Melody Carlson.
   pages ; cm
  ISBN 978-1-4555-2814-1 (paperback)—ISBN 978-1-4555-2813-4 (ebook)
  I. Title.
  PS3553.A73257Y68 2016
  813'.54—dc23   2015029425

Your Heart's Desire

Chapter 1

December 26, 1945

As the train left St. Paul station, Caroline Clark hoped she hadn't made an enormous mistake. What kind of mother pulls her son out of third grade in the middle of the school year, gives up a perfectly good job, abandons everything familiar, and relocates halfway across the country? Normal people just didn't do this sort of thing. Did they?

Caroline tugged at the cuff of a kid leather glove as she studied her son, trying to gauge his emotions as he stared out the window. Was he frightened like her, dreading the unknown? Miffed about leaving his school chums behind? Or perhaps he was simply curious about the speed of this sleek silver train, looking forward to the prospects of eating in the diner or sleeping in the upper berth tonight. She hoped his stoic expression was just suppressed excitement over this trip. And why shouldn't it be? Traveling more than two thousand miles from Minnesota to southern California—what young boy wouldn't love such an adventure?

She controlled the urge to smooth an unruly blond curl sticking straight out from the side of his cobalt-blue cap. It was an old habit that he'd politely but firmly asked her to abandon not so very long ago. Keeping her hands in her lap, she simply admired her little man. He looked so sweet in his Sunday suit. But the pant legs, which had been let out twice, were already too short again. He was growing up quickly. Too quickly, she was afraid. But Joseph had always been an old soul, wise beyond his years, even before his father died. Even so, was he truly ready for this? *Was she?*

Caroline glanced nervously at her watch. Normally, she would be behind her desk at this hour. She'd be finishing up the morning mail and looking forward to a coffee break and a friendly chat with Bernice. Working for the Northern Leather Company had been a big part of her life ever since Joe was killed in the South Pacific nearly four years ago. And she'd assumed she would continue working there until she was a very old lady. It had seemed the safe route.

Despite the freezing temperature outside, the train was already stuffy and warm. Caroline stood to remove her gray woolen coat, neatly folding it with the inside out and laying it on the empty seat across from them, next to her black leather handbag—a going-away gift from the leather company.

"Are you too warm?" she asked Joseph. He silently shook his head no. Still focused on the view from the window, he watched intently as the city buildings steadily melded into warehouses that slowly ran into urban neighborhoods. Not too unlike where she and Joseph used to live, except that their little apartment was on the other side of the city. Only six blocks down from her parents. She felt a lump in her throat to imagine what life would be without them so nearby. Who would Mom share coffee with on Saturday mornings?

"You're doing the right thing," her mother had insisted in late November, shortly after Caroline had informed her parents of her baby sister's interesting invitation. "Joseph will thrive in the warm California climate. Don't forget how bad his bronchitis got last winter, or the school days he missed."

"That's right," Dad had reassured her. "And if all goes well, your mother and I will join you girls out there by next year. Right after I retire."

"But what if I don't find a job?" Caroline questioned them.

"Of course you'll get a job," Dad had declared. "You've been a valuable employee at Northern Leather. Mark my words, the leather company will have its work cut out for it in finding a replacement for you."

As she reached for the *Life* magazine her mother had given her this morning, Caroline questioned her dad's confidence in her future employability. After all, he *was* her dad. It was only natural that he'd be biased in her favor. But what if he was wrong? What if she couldn't find a decent job? To distract herself from these dismal thoughts, she opened the magazine, flipping past a cigarette ad, and found herself staring at a headline that sent a chill down her spine. POSTWAR JOBS SCARCE FOR EVERYONE. It seemed to confirm the hopelessness of her situation, the folly of this trip.

Certainly, it was no secret that when the servicemen came home there weren't enough jobs to go around. Most of the women on the production line at the leather factory had been let go immediately. Most of the female secretaries were replaced with males, all war veterans. And if Caroline hadn't been a war widow herself, it was likely she'd have been jobless as well.

Was she a fool on a fool's errand? Dragging her poor son across the country, in the hopes of attaining a life that probably didn't even exist? Why hadn't she been more grateful for her old job? After all, she'd had a clean, warm office with relatively nice people to work with. And although her salary had been modest, it made life for her and Joseph a bit more comfortable. She'd even managed to stash away some savings—a nest egg that she was quickly depleting.

But thanks to her little sister's enticing letter last month, Caroline was turning her back on all of it. What *was* she thinking? She reached for her handbag, extracting the letter that she'd probably read a dozen times. Just for reassurance. She slowly unfolded it, skimming over the familiar words.

Dear Caroline,

First of all, I want to wish you Happy Thanksgiving. Lulu took her first steps last month. Danny is a handful, but at least he's in preschool three mornings a week. Rich got promoted to lead driver in the shipping department. That's partly why I'm writing you. Not to brag about Rich's promotion, but to tell you that the company he works for is expanding. According to Rich there are job opportunities. But more about that later.

The main reason I'm writing is to tell you about the house we signed papers on last week. Thanks to Rich's GI housing loan (and Rich's parents' generosity) we will move into our first real home next week. Four bedrooms! Can you believe it? And there's a brand-new school nearby. But the best news is that this house has a finished basement with a complete apartment that we plan to rent for additional income. I got to thinking it would be perfect for you and Joseph. And you could probably get a job where Rich works, at the chocolate factory. So, please, Sis, say yes. The climate here is wonderful. I know it will be good for Joseph's health. And my children really need their auntie. If you promise me that you'll pray about this idea, I will promise not to keep nagging you about it.

Love,
Marjorie

P.S. Don't tell Mom and Dad yet, but I'm expecting again. In June. I need my family nearby!

Caroline refolded the well-worn letter, slipping it back into her handbag. Although it was reassuring to have a place to stay, it wasn't as if Marjorie could offer them free rent. They clearly needed the rental income to help with their house payments. Just the same, it was a good opportunity. If only Caroline could land a decent job.

She looked back at Joseph, still glued to the window. "Are you having fun, honey?" she asked in a tentative tone, not certain she wanted to hear his honest response. What if he said no or that he was unhappy?

"Sure, Mom." He turned to give her a slightly somber-looking half smile.

"Are you excited about seeing your aunt and uncle and cousins?"

"I guess so."

"Are you sad that we left?" She braced herself for his answer.

He shrugged. "I'll miss my friends and school. And Grandma and Grandpa."

"Don't forget that Grandma and Grandpa want to relocate to California, too." She reached for the bag her mom had given her this morning. Mostly it was food and things for their trip. But she pulled out the book her dad had contributed. "This is a resource book about California," she told Joseph. "Grandpa thought you might like to read it during the trip." She opened it up to the first page, pointing to the beautiful photo of a white sandy beach peppered with colorful sun umbrellas and tanned people in swimwear. "Look at this, Joseph. Can you imagine what it will be like to swim in the ocean for the first time?"

He took the book, peering down into the photo with what seemed genuine interest. "The Pacific Ocean," he read out loud. "The California shoreline is 840 miles long." He looked impressed. "I bet Minnesota isn't even that long from one end to the other end."

"I'm pretty sure it's not," she told him.

As Joseph continued to read the book, sharing random tidbits of California information from time to time, she began to relax a little. Maybe he really was having a good time. And maybe she hadn't made such a ridiculous mistake after all. Besides, she reminded herself, she had done just as Marjorie had suggested. Caroline *had* prayed about this big decision. Right from the start, she had prayed long and hard. And it seemed like the doors had opened. In fact, after she gave notice at work, she'd had a real sense of peace about everything. And she couldn't wait to see Marjorie and the children. If she could only find a good job, it would be perfect. And she wouldn't even complain if the only work available was on the assembly line. In fact, she might actually welcome a job that didn't involve her secretarial skills. Besides, she'd always been quite fond of chocolate!

Chapter 2

Caroline couldn't believe how warm the air felt as she and Joseph emerged from the train car in Los Angeles. Also, despite it being nearly five o'clock, it seemed surprisingly light out. "I guess we don't need our overcoats after all," she said as she and Joseph carried their bags down the platform. Up ahead she spotted her sister, dressed in a stylish peach-colored suit and pushing a stroller. Beside her a little boy in short pants jumped up and down, waving both hands with enthusiasm.

"Our relatives!" Caroline said to Joseph as they hurried toward them.

"You're here at last!" Marjorie exclaimed as she embraced Caroline and Joseph. "I can hardly believe it!"

"Daddy's getting a cart for your suitcases," Danny informed Caroline.

"Wonderful." Caroline knelt to look in the small boy's big brown eyes. "Do you even remember me?"

"Yes," he told her. "You're Aunt Caroline. Mommy's sister. Mommy told me."

"And this is my son, Joseph," she said as Joseph stuck out his hand for a handshake. "Your cousin."

"You're big," Danny told Joseph. "How old are you?"

"Almost ten." Joseph stood taller with pride. "And you're four, right?"

Danny nodded.

"There's Rich now," Marjorie said. "Do you have more bags, Sis?"

Caroline pointed to where a pile of baggage was stacked on the platform. "We have a few other things in that pile and some larger trunks and things that I've arranged to have delivered to your house." She nudged Joseph as Marjorie's husband came along with a baggage cart. "Why don't you show Uncle Rich which bags are ours?"

"It's so warm here." Caroline removed her heavy coat, hanging it over her arm.

"Yes. It's warm for this time of year. More than seventy degrees today."

"Seventy degrees! And to think we left snow." Caroline knelt down to look at Lulu. "What a darling," she exclaimed. "A little living doll!" She peered up at Marjorie. "May I take her out of the stroller?"

"Of course! Just be careful if you let her down. That living doll has recently discovered she can run."

Caroline lifted Lulu out of the stroller, looking into her cherub face. "I'm your aunt Caroline," she said softly. "We've never met before."

Lulu made some happy babbles as she patted Caroline's cheeks.

"Here we go," Rich said as he and Joseph rolled the cart up

to them. "Everything present and accounted for?" He paused to give Caroline a welcome hug, then waited as she did a quick inventory of the cart, confirming that it was all there.

"And a few larger household items will be unloaded from a cargo car later. They'll be delivered to your house tomorrow," she explained as the five of them headed to the parking lot. "It's not that we brought a lot. Our other apartment was furnished."

"This one has a few furnishings," Marjorie explained as Rich opened the trunk of a late model Oldsmobile, starting to load it. "I'm afraid you'll need a few more things."

Caroline had assumed the basement apartment would be fully furnished, but kept this to herself. "What a beautiful car," she said as she ran her hand over the midnight-blue surface. It shone as if it had been recently waxed.

"Rich's parents got this," Marjorie told her. "Sort of a welcome home gift for Rich...you know, after he returned from the war."

Joseph's eyes grew large as he handed Rich a suitcase. Caroline could see he was impressed. She would have to explain to him that Rich's parents were very wealthy and, apparently, very generous, too. With the car's trunk nearly full, she took the smaller bags with her, waiting as Danny slid into the backseat. Then she and Joseph sat on either side, wedging their extra bags all around them like sardines.

"Mom," Joseph said urgently as Rich turned onto a wide street. "Look at those palm trees." He pointed out the window. "They look like something in a motion picture."

"My goodness," Caroline said with amazement. "I've never seen a real palm tree before."

"And flowers in the wintertime?" He pointed to a hedge with bright red blooms.

"Are those poinsettia plants?" she asked in wonder.

"Yes!" Marjorie exclaimed. "I nearly fainted when I saw them for the first time. Thousands of poinsettias. Honestly, it seemed decadent." She laughed. "But I suppose I've gotten used to it."

"Remember when Dad got Mom that poinsettia plant?" Caroline said.

"Yes. And the cold nearly killed it on his way home."

"And then it finally bloomed—one single flower."

"And we thought that was so wonderful." Marjorie laughed heartily.

"Oh, my." Caroline just shook her head at the multitude of red blooms. "I feel like I'm in a different country."

The sun was setting now, painting the sky in shades of rose and coral. Rich and Marjorie pointed out a few other interesting sights, but it was too much for Caroline to take in. The warm air, the bright flowers, a new life in a new city—she almost felt dizzy.

"That's our sign!" Danny leaned over a suitcase to point to the illuminated billboard. "Welcome to Golden Oaks!"

"You know how to read?" Joseph asked.

"He memorized that sign," Marjorie confided.

"Golden Oaks." Caroline repeated the magical-sounding name in wonder. Was she really going to live here? Make their home in Golden Oaks?

"Have you been here before?" Danny asked her.

"No, this is my first visit," she explained. "But your mom and I have been writing letters for years. She's told me a lot about it."

"I'll drive past the chocolate factory," Rich announced as he made a turn. "Just so you can see how close it is to our house."

"That sign says MG Chocolate Factory!" Danny proclaimed

as he pointed at the big brick building. "That's where my daddy works."

"You're certainly good at reading signs," Caroline told him. "So what does *MG* stand for?"

Danny shrugged. "I dunno. But they make good chocolate."

"Maybe it stands for Mighty Good," Joseph suggested.

"MG is for Maxwell Gordon," Rich said as he stopped for the traffic light. "It used to be called Maxwell Gordon Fine Chocolates, but they shortened it. Mr. Gordon founded the company more than forty years ago. I should say he and his wife founded it. It started out as a tiny fudge shop in Los Angeles."

"Mr. Gordon is retired now," Marjorie continued. "His son Max Jr. took over for, uh, a while...until the other brother stepped in."

"The *other brother* is doing an impressive job," Rich added.

"He's Golden Oaks' most wealthy and eligible bachelor." Marjorie giggled. "Or so I've heard."

"Maybe Caroline will snag him," Rich said.

"Goodness, no!" Caroline exclaimed.

"Oh, don't pay Rich any mind. He's just a big tease," Marjorie told her.

"Sorry," Rich said quickly. "I forgot you haven't been around me much."

"Besides, any woman wanting to land that man would have her work cut out for her. One of my girlfriends calls him Mr. Untouchable."

"That sounds about right." Rich laughed. "But Mr. Untouchable draws women like an old fish creel draws flies." As the light turned green, he pointed out a small shop. With candy-striped awnings, it appeared to be attached to

the larger factory building. "That's the storefront shop for
MG Chocolates. It was built to resemble the original one, but
it's about five times bigger. It actually serves both as a retail
chocolate shop and a showroom. MG stocks everything that
the company makes in there."

"Yummy." Danny smacked his lips. "Can we go inside,
Daddy?"

"I'm sure they're closed by now," Rich told him.

"Besides, I've got dinner in the oven. And I'm sure Aunt
Caroline and Joseph would like to get settled after their long
train trip," Marjorie added.

"Our house is only eight blocks away from the chocolate
factory," Rich explained as he turned onto a side street. "I usually walk to work."

"That way I get to have the car during the day," Marjorie
said.

"That's a handy setup." Caroline studied the pretty tree-
lined street. "I always took the bus to work." One more thing
she would not miss.

"Well, if you get hired at MG, you can walk to work, too."
Rich slowed the car.

"Do you really think I can get a job?" she asked him as
he turned into the driveway of a pale yellow two-story stucco
house.

"They posted six openings on the assembly line, and that's
this past week alone."

"What a gorgeous house," Caroline exclaimed as they all
got out of the car. "I love the ironwork. It looks like we could
be somewhere in Spain."

"Mediterranean," Marjorie said as she set Lulu down on the
grass. "Danny, you keep an eye on your sister while we unload
Aunt Caroline's things."

"Why don't you ladies go inside," Rich suggested. "The boys and I can handle this."

"Thanks," Marjorie called out as Lulu took off running across the lawn. "Hopefully the meatloaf isn't all dried out. I left it in the oven."

"I'll grab my niece." Caroline hurried to scoop up Lulu. "Are you going to show me your room, Lulu? I'll bet it's a pretty one."

"Rich's dad has been helping me to paint. Everything was such dull, dreary colors." Marjorie opened the front door.

"How nice of him." Caroline went inside.

"He's retired and says it gives him something to do. We're not completely done yet, but it's getting better. And the kids' rooms are all set."

"What a lovely room!" Caroline looked around the spacious living room with its large front windows. There was a small brown couch against one wall and a well-worn easy chair against another.

"It is lovely, but it desperately needs more furniture." Marjorie waved her hand across the slightly barren space. "I can't even imagine how I'll begin to fill it up."

"One piece at a time." Caroline set Lulu down.

"You sound like Rich." Marjorie made a pouting expression.

"Well, as our mother likes to say, 'Rome wasn't built in a day.'"

"But it would be so nice to have some more pieces for people to sit on, don't you think? I mean if we ever have guests. New Year's Eve is just a few days away. It would've been fun to have a party. Not this year."

Caroline pointed to the lushly carpeted floor. "Get some big pillows. Let people sit on them Bohemian style."

"Really?" Marjorie looked skeptical. "I want to show you the rest of the place, but I need to check the meatloaf first." She led them through a somewhat formal dining room with a metal chandelier. A small plastic-topped kitchen table and four metal chairs seemed slightly out of place, but Caroline didn't plan to mention it.

"Smells good," Caroline said as she followed Marjorie into the kitchen.

"I used Mom's recipe—the one with mashed potatoes on top."

"Wonderful." Caroline looked down at the green linoleum floor. "Especially after three days of train food."

"Three days of someone else doing the cooking sounds like a welcome vacation to me." Marjorie checked the oven, then turned on the burner beneath a saucepan.

"Your kitchen is very nice." Caroline ran her hand over a white cabinet door. "It looks recently painted."

"Yes." Marjorie pointed to the shell-pink wall. "But Rich doesn't like the wall color. He says it looks too girlish." She giggled. "Probably because it's the same color I used to paint Lulu's room. But it's not like he spends much time in here anyway."

Marjorie continued the house tour. "This is the downstairs bathroom," she said proudly. "I never dreamed I'd have a house with *two* bathrooms." She opened the door to reveal a small bathroom. "Of course, it doesn't have a tub or shower. The real estate agent called it a half-bath. I haven't decided what color to paint it yet, but this boring beige has to go."

"Very handy." Caroline nodded. "Especially for a big family."

Marjorie balanced Lulu on her hip as she led Caroline up the stairs. "This is Danny's room." She opened the door to reveal a bright blue room furnished with a neatly made bed and a small dresser, a bookshelf, toy chest, and child-sized wooden rocking chair. It was charming. The next bedroom was Lulu's. Like the kitchen it was shell pink and very girlish looking with white ruffled curtains. Next she led them into a sparsely furnished, but larger, room. The walls were robin's egg blue, giving it a peaceful feeling. "This is our bedroom," Marjorie told her. "I painted it all by myself. I mixed leftover paint from Danny's room with some white to make the color."

"It's a beautiful shade of blue," Caroline said. "And you did a good job. I never knew my sister was a painter."

"It's really pretty easy. That reminds me—I saved some leftover paint in case you want to try your hand in the apartment."

"I've never really painted much, but it might be fun. And you've done such a great job in these rooms. You're an inspiration."

Marjorie beamed at her. "Oh, I'm so glad you're here, Caroline. I've been just dying to show this house to my family. I've been working so hard on it. Our first home."

"And it's all just wonderful." Caroline smiled at her baby sister, remembering how Marjorie used to love playing with baby dolls and the dollhouse as a child. In some ways, she hadn't changed much. "You're very blessed, you know."

"I know." Marjorie straightened her comb-and-brush set on the dresser. "It's just so fun to share it with my family. Rich's parents come over a lot, and they've been really helpful. But I've missed having my own family." She showed Caroline the guest room. "It's a mess with my sewing stuff, but I want to fix it all up for the folks...for when they come out. Mom said maybe by summer. Won't that be great?"

"It's so nice you have all this space." Caroline's previous apartment had only one tiny bedroom that had been used by

Joseph. She'd slept on the sofa bed. She was curious about the downstairs apartment, but knew the time would come to see it. "You have a lovely home and a lovely family, Marjorie. You're truly blessed."

"I hear the boys coming in." Marjorie opened another door. "The upstairs bathroom." She stepped back to allow Caroline to enter. "Can you believe how roomy it is?"

"It's huge." Caroline looked around the pale-green-tiled space in wonder. Not only did it have a generous-sized bathtub, but a separate shower as well. The sink vanity ran the length of the room, and the toilet had its own separate door. "I've never seen such an enormous bathroom."

"I guess they're more common here in California," Marjorie explained as she plucked up Lulu to keep her from climbing into the bathtub. The disgruntled child kicked and twisted in her arms. "At least in bigger homes anyway."

"Well, it's all very, very nice," Caroline proclaimed. "I'm so happy for you and Rich. You're very fortunate." Despite her cheerful words, Caroline felt a strange twinge inside of her. Something akin to jealousy, and that was disturbing. Because, really, she was happy for her younger sister. On closer examination, she decided this feeling was more like regret…or longing. Like a question that had been nesting in some recess of her mind. A question she never wanted to fully face. As they headed for the staircase, the troublesome question hit Caroline without warning: *What would her life be like right now if Joe hadn't been killed in the war?*

"Want to go to Aunt Caroline?" Marjorie held out the fussing toddler.

Caroline reached for Lulu. "Come on, sweetie pie." To her relief, Lulu outstretched her arms. "That's the girl." She ran her hand over Lulu's thick auburn curls. Like Caroline, she must've inherited that from their grandmother's side of the family.

"I better get dinner on the table." Marjorie led the way down the stairs.

"Do you worry about Lulu falling on the stairs?" Caroline asked.

"Yes. I never let her out of my sight." Marjorie stopped at the foot of the stairs. "I've seen those gates that keep toddlers away from the stairway. I think I'll have to look into one soon. Especially with a new baby coming."

"Sounds like a very good idea."

Marjorie let out a loud sigh as she led them back to the kitchen. "I know Rich is working as hard as he can. And he's even gotten a couple of raises. But it's so hard to furnish a big house like this. His mom has offered to help, but Rich put his foot down. He says they've done enough and I'm not allowed to accept any more gifts from them."

Caroline nodded. "They have been very generous."

"Rich acts like he doesn't care about material things. He keeps telling me to take it slowly. But I want it all." She laughed. "And I want it right now."

Caroline chuckled. That sounded like the baby sister she'd grown up with. Marjorie had always been impatient. And perhaps a bit spoiled, too. But she was basically good-hearted. Caroline remembered when Marjorie had insisted on coming out to California. She was so certain that she'd be discovered as the next Ginger Rogers. As soon as she'd turned eighteen, she had taken off. And, although the movie star thing never worked out, it hadn't turned out too badly for her. Not at all. And, really, Caroline was happy for her.

Chapter 3

Caroline would never say so, but Marjorie's meatloaf was nothing like their mother's. To be fair, it was probably Caroline's fault—since dinner had been delayed by the trip to the train station. "Let me clear," Caroline offered as they finished up dinner.

"But you're the guest," Marjorie argued. "And you already helped put Lulu to bed for me."

"I'm also your sister," Caroline reminded her. "And remember Mom's rules. The cook shouldn't have to clean up."

Marjorie laughed as she handed Caroline her plate. "Fine. You win, Sis."

Caroline pointed to Joseph now. "Has Danny shown you his room yet?"

Joseph just shrugged.

"He had some interesting-looking toy planes," Caroline said enticingly.

"Come on, Joseph," Danny urged. "Come see my room. We can play."

As Joseph reluctantly followed his cousin, Caroline finished clearing the table. With a load of dishes in her hands, she grinned at her sister and Rich. "Looks like it's just the two of you for a bit. Better enjoy it."

Rich chuckled. "What a novelty."

Caroline was glad to busy herself in the kitchen. Her plan was to quickly finish in here, then to get downstairs to see that apartment. Rich had already put their things down there, but she was eager to get her and Joseph settled. Anxious to see their new home, she figured that if the basement was anything like the rest of this house, it would be a huge improvement.

"You're quick," Marjorie said when she came in to see Caroline putting the last of the clean dishes in the cupboard. "Rich wants some coffee to go with dessert."

"Dessert?" Caroline looked around the kitchen.

Marjorie chuckled. "Actually, I didn't make dessert. But we always have chocolate tucked somewhere." She opened a high cupboard, removing a plain-looking box. "Employees are allowed to buy seconds for wholesale." She opened the box to show Caroline.

"Seconds? They look perfectly fine."

"It has to do with the swirls and markings on the tops of the chocolates. I haven't figured it all out yet, but each design signifies different fillings. If the swirls aren't perfect, they wind up in the reject boxes—becoming seconds."

"Interesting." Caroline closed the dish cupboard.

"Would you like coffee, too?"

"That sounds good, but do you mind if I go take a peek at the apartment first?"

Marjorie slapped her forehead. "I'm sorry—I forgot you hadn't seen it."

"It's okay. I'm just curious. And I'd like to start unpacking."

"Of course." She set down the coffeepot. "Let me take you—"

"You go ahead and make coffee. Just point the way."

"Certainly." Marjorie led Caroline through the laundry room and opened a door. "This is one way to get down there. And there's an outside entrance as well—that's the door Rich and Joseph used to put your things inside. Go ahead and check it out. And my apologies that it's not in better shape. I've been so busy with the rest of the house and the children...well, hopefully it's not too bad down there." She flipped a light switch to illuminate a rather steep-looking wooden staircase.

Caroline thanked her and carefully proceeded down, and finding another light switch at the foot of the stairs, she clicked it on to reveal a small kitchen and connected living area. Like her sister had said, it was partially furnished, but the few furnishings looked old and dusty, and besides a worn sofa and wooden rocker, the rest would probably be better off in a junkyard.

Still, with a thorough cleaning and some fresh air, the space should be fine. And perhaps she could make a slipcover for the sofa. Marjorie wasn't the only one who could sew. In fact, between the two of them—when they were growing up—Caroline was the one who really knew her way around a needle and thread.

She went into the kitchen, turning on the overhead light. The cabinets were a dull shade of yellow—although on closer inspection, they simply appeared to be dirty. Perhaps some elbow grease and a good scrub would revive them a bit. She

continued inspecting the dreary space, shaking her head over
things that should've been thrown out after the last tenant
left...whenever that was.

Certainly, it was dismal, but with a little work and imagination, she could probably change that. She opened the door
to the grimy bathroom and almost fell over from the smell.
Fine, make that a *lot* of work!

Fortunately, the small bedrooms—and to her delight
there were two of them—were in better shape. Each one
contained a twin bed—and the mattresses appeared to
be brand new. That was a huge relief. Caroline went to
look through the bags that Rich had stacked by the door.
Unless she was mistaken, one of these cases contained bed-
ding. It was reassuring to know that she and Joseph would
at least have a fairly comfortable place to sleep. That was
something.

Hearing her sister calling that dessert was ready, Caroline
hurried back up the steep staircase to join them.

"The boys are playing so nicely upstairs that I decided not
to bother them," Marjorie said as she set a plate of chocolates
on the table where their coffee cups and saucers were already
waiting.

"How did you like the apartment?" Rich asked as Marjorie
went back for the coffeepot. Caroline could tell by his expression that he was concerned.

"I think it has good potential," Caroline said carefully.
"Will you mind if I don't use all the furnishings?"

"Not at all. You pick out what you want to use, and the
rest can go to the dump."

"And I was really pleased to see that the mattresses in the
bedrooms are new."

"The ones that were here before looked awful." He lowered

his voice. "Stein's Furniture had a sale right after Christmas and I thought it was the least I could do."

"What did you do?" Marjorie asked as she filled up Caroline's coffee cup with arched brows.

"I, uh, I got new mattresses for the apartment."

Marjorie stopped pouring to stare at him. "But I thought you said we couldn't afford to buy any—"

"The mattresses down there were absolutely horrible, Marjorie. You couldn't expect a dog to—"

"I know, but you said—"

"Did you really expect Caroline and Joseph to sleep on them?" His voice grew louder.

Marjorie glared at him. "Well, you could've at least told me. It's not as if I—"

"Why don't you let me pay you for them?" Caroline offered. "Since they're for Joseph and me. It seems only fair."

Rich frowned. "That wasn't what I intended."

"Please." Caroline smiled warmly at him. "I *want* to pay for them. I have a small budget for getting the apartment set up. And it's wonderful you were able to find them at a reduced price. Very helpful."

Rich held up his hands as if to surrender. "How about if I let you sisters figure these things out from now on?"

"Good thinking." Marjorie filled his cup and then her own.

"I really do appreciate that you're both welcoming me into your home," Caroline said pleasantly. "And I'm eager to roll up my sleeves and make that apartment a home for Joseph and me."

Marjorie scrunched her nose as she passed the chocolate plate to Caroline. "I hope you weren't too discouraged by the condition of the place."

"It didn't seem like anything that some soap and water

couldn't fix." Caroline took a chocolate. "And until I get myself a real job, I'll consider getting that apartment cleaned up as Job One."

"Just make sure you get your application in at MG as soon as possible," Rich warned her. "The more that people hear about the benefits and great working conditions there, the more competitive it gets."

"I plan to go in first thing on Monday," she assured him.

"That's New Year's Eve," Marjorie pointed out. "Are they open?"

"Of course," Rich told her. "This is MG's biggest season ever. We're getting so many orders for Valentine's Day that Mr. Gordon is considering staying in production on Saturdays, too."

"Does that mean you, too?" Marjorie looked worried.

He grinned. "Now that I'm only driving the California circuit, I probably won't ever have to work on Saturday. At least for the most part."

"That's a relief."

"Do you like driving a delivery truck?" Caroline asked hesitantly. She knew it was probably nosy to inquire, but her parents had been curious about this for some time. Rich was the only son of a very wealthy family, and he'd been halfway through college when he'd given it all up.

"I love driving and being on the road. It feels like real freedom. Sort of like being a cowboy. And, yeah, I'm aware that some people scratch their heads over it...they think I should strive for something more. But the truth is I was never a bookish guy. Not even in college. I couldn't wait to quit school so I could join the Flying Tigers. My folks thought I was being a hero."

"So did I." Marjorie smiled.

He turned to her. "And then I let this little girl turn my head. I suppose the die was cast when I got hitched before I

joined up." He reached over to squeeze her hand. "But no regrets there."

"None for me either." She beamed at him. "No regrets
whatsoever."

He looked deeply into her eyes as he continued to hold
her hand. "You honestly don't feel bad about not having that
wonderful acting career you'd hoped for?"

Marjorie laughed. "Well, if I feel bad, I'm in good company. Me and about a million other delusional girls who came
out here with movie star dreams. We've all had to figure out
another way to live."

"So you're really happy?"

"I am." She leaned forward and they exchanged a sweet kiss.

Caroline glanced away, preparing an excuse to leave the
happy couple alone, but before she could even stand, the boys
came barreling into the room.

"*Chocolate!*" Danny declared, his eyes eager.

"Just one," his mother told him. "With a glass of milk."

"Can Joseph have one, too?" Danny asked innocently.

Marjorie patted Danny on the cheek. "Joseph can have two."

"Why does he get—"

"Because he's twice as big as you." Marjorie pointed to the
bathroom. "Now go wash your hands and I'll get both you
boys a glass of milk."

While the rest of them were scurrying about, Caroline
turned to Rich. "I really do appreciate you getting those mattresses for us. It was very thoughtful."

He smiled. "And I'm really glad you and Joseph are here,
Caroline. I think it'll be good for all of us."

On Saturday morning, Caroline felt torn. On one hand, she
wanted to spend time with Marjorie and her family. On the

other hand, she wanted to use this day to get Joseph and her somewhat settled. At the moment it felt more like camping than real living. So when she woke early, even before the sun was up, she took careful inventory of the sadly neglected apartment, peeking into cabinets and cupboards and creating a long to-do list.

"I have lots of errands and chores today," she told Joseph as she sat on the edge of his bed later that morning. "You can come with me and help if you like. Or you can stay here at Aunt Marjorie's. I'm sure she wouldn't mind. Especially if you help out with your cousins."

"I'll stay here," he said sleepily.

Then, still wearing her pajamas and robe, she crept up the stairs to find Marjorie, also in her pajamas, warming a bottle for Lulu in the kitchen.

"Good morning," Caroline said. "I wasn't sure you'd be up yet. I mean since it's Saturday."

Marjorie blinked sleepily at Caroline. "I'm up because Lulu is up. But why are you up? I figured you'd be exhausted after your long trip."

"I woke up full of energy." Caroline quickly explained her plan. "If you don't mind, Joseph would like to stick around this morning. He promised to help with Danny and Lulu if you need it."

Marjorie's eyes lit up. "Sounds good to me."

"I should be back by noon or sooner."

"Where are you going?"

"I noticed some shops as we drove through town last night," Caroline said. "I need to pick up a few necessities, you know, for the apartment. I've made a list. And I thought I should lay in some food provisions as well."

"Oh, yeah, sure." Marjorie turned off the burner and, removing the bottle, tested it on her wrist with a weak smile. "I know, I know, Lulu is old enough to drink cold milk now. At least that's what one of the parenting journals says. But she still likes it warmed."

Caroline placed a hand on Marjorie's shoulder. "You're a good mom."

"Really?" Her blue eyes grew big. "You think so?"

"I know so."

As Caroline walked down the tree-lined street, she could feel a bounce in her step. It was hard to fully grasp everything, but it felt as if she were in the right place at the right time—and it felt good. Of course, it didn't hurt that the sun was shining, or that she'd fled the land of winter to arrive in the land of springtime. Besides that, she had a happy anticipation for what lay ahead today.

She'd dressed relatively casually for her errands. Not trousers, although she'd wanted to, but being new in town—and new to California life—she felt she should dress for the occasion. And a work suit seemed a bit over the top. So she'd worn a dress she'd made for herself last summer. The first new thing she'd had since the war began. It was only a simple shirtwaist dress in a practical gray-and-white-checked fabric, with a little white collar. Over her shoulders, she'd draped a gray cashmere sweater (a thoughtful Christmas gift from her parents) not because she was cold, but simply because it was almost January and to go without outerwear seemed shocking. Besides, the soft sweater felt luxurious.

She had numerous items on her list, and doubted she could accomplish everything today, but determined to try. Mostly she was grateful for the ground beneath her feet (not the rumbling train) and she was eager to get acquainted with Golden Oaks. She knew from what Marjorie had told her that the population was just under twenty thousand. Very small compared to what she was used to, but big enough to have some interesting businesses. And because it was a bedroom city to Los Angeles, she suspected Golden Oaks was much more cosmopolitan than a town of similar size in Minnesota. She wanted to walk around and imagine what it would feel like to be a real citizen here.

It was interesting to see the tidy little town in the morning light. And staggering to see that flowerpots were in full bloom! Most of the buildings seemed relatively new, as if this town had sprouted up in the twentieth century. The chocolate company appeared to be one of the oldest ones, and the brass sign in front said: COMPANY FOUNDED IN 1903—FACTORY BUILT IN 1913. She peered in the front window of the factory, but it looked dark and quiet inside. Even the cute little retail shop next to it was closed. She read the sign on the door, discovering that, like most of the other shops and stores, it didn't open until ten on Saturdays.

And since it was barely past nine, she decided to buy a newspaper from the newsstand and try out Dee Dee's Coffee Shop. Dee Dee's was just one block down from the chocolate factory, and judging from the traffic going in and out, it was a busy place. She waited her turn to order her coffee and butterhorn, then carried them to the only unoccupied table. Proceeding to make herself comfortable, she opened her paper and read the front page, then skimmed the following pages, before finally settling into the employment section of the classified ads. With a pencil handy to circle anything of interest, she studied the first ad with care. It was for an accountant, and although she'd had one bookkeeping class in secretarial school, she did not feel it was her strong suit.

"Excuse me," a male voice said.

She looked up to see an attractive dark-haired man smiling down on her. Dressed casually in tan trousers and a dark blue knit shirt, it was his disarming smile that made her catch her breath. *"Yes?"*

"Do you mind if I sit here for a bit?" He nodded to where the rest of the small coffee shop was packed full. "Until another table opens up."

"Not at all." She gave him a polite but slightly nervous smile. "I felt a little guilty taking this big table all to myself, but it was the only one left. Please, make yourself at home."

"Thank you." He sat down in the chair to her right and removed the first section of a much bulkier newspaper than the local one she had opened. She peered to see it was the *Los Angeles Times*. Leaning back in the straight-back chair, the handsome stranger took a relaxed sip of his coffee as he gazed at the front page. She was tempted to read the headline, but knew that was rude. And why was she staring at him? What was wrong with her anyway?

Feeling silly and slightly unsettled, she attempted to refocus her attention on the employment ads, but there was no denying that this attractive gentleman was proving a major distraction. That in itself was curious, since she'd never wasted much time concerning herself with men in general—not in the last decade anyway. And if anyone ever asked, she clearly communicated that she had no interest in dating...and no intentions of ever marrying again—period. But at the moment she felt strangely obsessed with trying to get a glimpse of this stranger's left hand. Curious as to whether his ring finger was occupied or not. Although that seemed rather ridiculous considering that her own ring finger, currently concealed by her newspaper, still displayed the gold band that Joe had given her back in 1934.

Stop it—stop it—stop it! She silently scolded herself for being such a nitwit. Then, fixing her attention back onto the employment ads, she used her pencil to circle a large help-wanted ad without even reading it. Simply to appear preoccupied.

"Hunting for a job?" he asked.

She turned to look at him, but when their eyes locked, she grew as tongue-tied and awkward as a schoolgirl. "Uh, yes," she stammered, "as a matter of fact, I am."

He laid down his newspaper with an apologetic smile. "Sorry, I didn't mean to be a busybody. I just noticed you were reading the employment ads. Excuse me for intruding."

"That's okay." She smiled meekly.

With a doubtful look, he reached over and pointed to the ad she'd just circled. "You, uh, have mechanical experience?"

Now she peered more closely at the ad. It was for a garage mechanic. She laughed in embarrassment. "Oh, dear! Silly me." She crossed the ad out, then shook her head. "I must be tired." She picked up her coffee and, taking a slow sip, willed herself to become invisible. A garage mechanic—*really?*

"Are you new in town?" He leaned forward slightly.

"Fresh off the train." She quickly explained how she'd just arrived last night. "All the way from Minnesota. Three days, two nights. Some people say they sleep marvelously on trains, but I'm not one of them."

"I never sleep well on trains, either."

"Joseph had no problem whatsoever. He slept like a baby." She saw the question in his eyes. "Uh, Joseph is my son. He's with me," she rambled nervously. "Well, not *here* with me.

He's with my sister and her husband at the moment. I came to town to look around and do some shopping." She felt even sillier now. Why was she going on like this?

"I see..."

She took in a deep breath. "Sorry...I didn't mean to give you my whole personal history. I suppose I'm still feeling a bit sleep-deprived."

"But you *are* looking for a job?"

She made a stiff smile. "Yes, I am. But not as a car mechanic." Her smile became uncomfortable. "The truth is I'm not even a very good driver."

To her relief he laughed.

"I need to find work as soon as possible," she confessed. "My brother-in-law works for MG Chocolates and he says they're hiring right now, and that I might possibly get a job on the assembly line."

"Have you worked an assembly line before?"

"No." She smiled sheepishly. "But I like chocolate."

He laughed again, and she felt herself relaxing a bit more.

"I actually worked as a stenographer. You see, I did a full secretarial course and worked for an insurance company until I married." She paused, wondering why she was telling him all this, but he did seem interested. "After that I had a very good secretarial job at a Minneapolis factory." She sighed. "I'd been there nearly five years, throughout the war."

"Laid off because of the returning servicemen?" His expression looked sympathetic.

"Actually I was one of the few women *not* laid off," she confided. "I quit my job when we decided to come out here."

"I see..."

"I hope I didn't do it backward though."

"Backward?"

"Yes. I keep wondering if I should've secured a job out here before giving up the one back there. You know the old saying, a bird in the hand..." She frowned. "I was just reading an article in *Life* magazine. Jobs are scarcer than ever."

"Over all, I'm sure that jobs are scarce. But opportunities vary from region to region. And you're right about MG Chocolates. We are hiring for the assembly line."

"*We?*" She studied him closely. "You work there, too?"

"Yes." He nodded.

"I suspect you don't work on the assembly line." Of course, as soon as she said this, she regretted it. People took all kinds of jobs these days. Work was work and you were lucky if you could get it. Who was she to judge?

"I've worked the line before."

"Really?" She blinked in surprise.

"As a matter of fact, I got rather good at it. You have to have fast hands and a quick mind." He studied her. "Do you think you'd have those skills?"

She set the newspaper aside to look down at her hands, spreading her fingers. "Well, I can type pretty fast, and that takes some quick thinking. But to be honest, I'm not sure how that would translate to an assembly line."

"Well, you never know until you try." He took a sip of coffee, glancing over his shoulder.

"Right. And if I don't find something else...something more suitable to my training and background..." She shrugged. "Well, the assembly line would be better than nothing." She wanted to add that she would do almost anything to support herself and her son, but knew that would sound desperate...and pathetic.

"Then I suggest you get your application in as soon as possible. I hear they've received quite a stack already."

"I plan to go in first thing on Monday."

"Good luck with that." He pointed to a small table on the other side of the coffee shop that had just vacated. "And now I will leave you to your paper and your peace." He tipped his head politely. "Thank you."

She picked up her paper, but peace was nowhere to be found now. Something about that man, the way he questioned her, the way he looked at her, well, it just made her uncomfortable. Too familiar...too personal...too disconcerting. And she didn't even know his name! If this was how people—particularly male people—behaved out here in California, well, maybe she was in the wrong place!

Chapter 4

Caroline pushed thoughts of the disturbing stranger from her mind as she strolled up and down Main Street, going from store to shop, visiting with the various businesses as she attempted to locate the miscellaneous items on her list. From basic cleaning supplies to slipcover fabric, table lamps to area rugs, it felt like she needed a little bit of everything. And to her relief the small town of Golden Oaks seemed to have it.

By noon she had unearthed all sorts of treasure and most items on her list were crossed off. Not only that, but many of the shops, when they discovered she was on foot, arranged for free delivery later in the day. Her last stop was at the grocery store, where she pulled out another list. When she discovered their delivery service was free for anyone with a revolving account, she agreed, gratefully handing the young man her rather large list. As he made a rounded tally, she filled out the form for her account.

"We'll get that to you around three," he said as she handed him a check. As he made her a receipt, she totaled what remained in her checkbook, trying not to cringe at the surprisingly low number—hoping she'd made a mistake.

As she walked back home, she mentally retraced her spending. It wasn't as if she hadn't been frugal. She had! She'd shopped for bargains and asked about discounts. And the larger purchases, like the dresser for Joseph and a small kitchen table and two chairs and a few other items, had all been from a nicely run secondhand store.

However, her nest egg had taken a beating. And, although she'd given herself a fairly strict budget, which included what she'd set aside to repay Rich for the new mattresses, she wasn't sure there was enough left over to tide her and Joseph by until she secured a job—and a paycheck. Suddenly the idea of working on an assembly line or even as a car mechanic didn't sound so terrible. When times were hard—and she'd certainly been through plenty of them—you simply did what you had to do. And you prayed a lot.

"There you are," Marjorie said happily as Caroline walked across the yard with her arms full of bags and packages. "What on earth have you got there?"

"Just a few things for the apartment." Caroline set a bag next to the exterior entrance to the basement apartment and came over to where Marjorie was sitting on the front porch steps, sunning her legs, which already looked golden tan.

"Well, your trunks and things were delivered from the train station just a little bit ago. I had the men put them inside your door. Don't trip over them. And I put the extra paint I told you about down there. As well as paintbrushes and some old sheets I was using for drop cloths and a few other things."

"Thanks." Caroline looked around the yard. "Where are the kids?"

"Lulu is napping. And Joseph is reading to Danny. And when he's finished, Danny is supposed to take a nap, too." She sighed happily. "My favorite time of day. And even better with Joseph here to help out. I'm tempted to steal that boy from you, Caroline. He is a gem."

Caroline smiled. "I know."

"And Danny just adores him."

"I'm so glad."

"Well, you probably want to go put your packages away." Marjorie stifled a yawn. "And I might just grab a nap myself."

"Sounds like a good idea." Caroline nodded. "I remember how tired I would get when I was expecting Joseph. I can't imagine how much more exhausting it must be to have two little ones to chase with a new one on the way."

"You got that right." Marjorie brightened as she slowly stood. "And that reminds me of something. Can I ask you a favor, Caroline?"

"Of course."

"Well, it's been ages and ages since Rich and I have gone out. You know, just the two of us together. Like a date. And I realized this morning that it won't be too long before I won't fit into a nice evening dress and—"

"I would love to watch your kids for you tonight," Caroline offered.

"You would?"

"Absolutely. You two go out and have a good time." She set down her packages and reached for her handbag. "And that reminds me." She pulled out a check. "This is for the mattresses. Tell me if it's not enough. And tell Rich they are very comfortable and we're so grateful."

Marjorie threw her arms around Caroline. "You are the best sister in the whole world. I have missed you so much!"

"I missed you, too." Caroline held her close.

"How does seven sound?" Marjorie asked. "I mean for us to go out? Will that work for you?"

"Seven is great." Caroline started gathering up her packages again. "That'll give me time to get a few things done in there."

"I'm going to call and see if I can get reservations for the new dinner club. It opened up before Christmas. It's called Parisian Moonlight." She sighed. "Doesn't that sound romantic? Dinner and dancing...oh, I can hardly wait!"

Marjorie happily went into the house, and Caroline carried her purchases into the apartment. Unfortunately, the apartment looked even more dismal than she remembered and the air smelled worse than Joseph's smelliest tennis shoes. But as she changed into dungarees and an old plaid shirt that Joe used to call his "Saturday shirt," she reassured herself that this was a temporary problem. Nothing a little elbow grease and strong soap wouldn't solve. Squinting to see her reflection in the murky bathroom mirror, she tied a protective scarf around her hair, imagining how much better the little apartment could look when she was finished. What a great way to show her appreciation to Marjorie and Rich.

Before unpacking her cleaning supplies, she opened the few small windows and the screen door. Then she rolled up her sleeves. Her first task was to attack the disgusting bathroom. As she scrubbed down the shower stall she was surprised to discover that the tiles were actually white, not dingy gray. And the sink and toilet turned out to be white as well. She was just done washing down the last wall when she heard Joseph calling for her.

"I'm in here," she yelled back.

"What're you doing?" he asked.

She stifled the urge to be sarcastic. "Cleaning." She stood up straight, dropping the washrag into the bucket of dirty water and surveying her work. "What do you think?"

"Looks better." He ran a finger over the shining white porcelain sink. "I didn't want to say anything, but it was kind of scary looking last night."

"I have to agree with you." She ruffled his blond curls. "I hear you've been really helpful with Danny today. Thanks."

"He's a funny little kid, but I kind of like him." Joseph leaned against the counter with a surprisingly mature expression. "He's asleep now."

"Did you have lunch?"

"Yeah. Aunt Marjorie made us peanut butter sandwiches and milk."

"I figured she'd feed you." She pushed a stray lock of hair back under her scarf.

"You need any help, Mom?"

"Really?" She peered into his face. "You *want* to help?"

"I don't mind."

She looked around the tiny bathroom. "How do you feel about painting?"

"Painting?" His eyes grew wide. "You mean the walls?"

She pointed to the wall she'd just cleaned. Although it looked better, it was a grungy shade of beige and rather splotchy. "Do you think you'd be a very good painter?"

He shrugged. "I helped paint that mural at my school. Remember?"

"I do remember. It was nice."

"Seems like painting a wall with just one color would be easier."

"Do you want to try?"

His eyes lit up. *"Yeah!"*

It wasn't long until they both decided the aqua-blue paint would be nice in the bathroom. Then they discussed how to use the drop cloth and a few other things, including a wooden box for him to stand on to reach higher. Caroline offered to get the highest sections. And thanks to his school mural experience, Joseph seemed to understand the basics of painting even better than she did. After he changed into some old clothes, Caroline simply stepped back and let him go at it. But as she watched him dipping a brush into the paint can she felt guilty. Sure, he was mature for his age and wanted to help, but shouldn't an almost ten-year-old be outside? "Are you certain you want to do this?" she asked one more time.

"Yeah, Mom." He didn't even look up as he brushed a wide stripe of aqua-blue paint on the wall next to the toilet. "This is fun!"

"Well, if it's too hard, just quit," she told him as she moved away from the doorway. "Yell if you need help."

He continued brushing the paint on, making the swath wider. "I like this, Mom. Really. Look how good that color looks."

She chuckled to herself as she remembered Tom Sawyer and the whitewashed picket fence. Hopefully she hadn't tricked Joseph into this. "Well, I'll understand if you change your mind. In the meantime, I'll be cleaning the kitchen."

For the next hour or so, they both worked quietly. She was nearly done cleaning the tiny kitchen when she heard someone calling through the screen door. "Grocery delivery for Mrs. Clark."

"I'm coming," she yelled as she ran to let the young man inside, warning him to watch his step as he carried the big box inside.

"Put it there," she pointed to the still damp countertop.

He set it down, then looked around the disheveled place with a puzzled expression. "You really live in this?"

"We're just moving in," she explained. "It's still a little messy."

He frowned. "And small."

"Yes, well, it's big enough. Here, let me get you a tip."

He held up his hands. "No, that's okay, ma'am."

"But I—"

"Maybe next time." And just like that he hurried away.

Caroline chuckled to herself as she imagined how this place must've seemed to the young man. He probably refused his tip because he figured they were very impoverished and desperately in need of every penny. That was actually very sweet and, in some ways, not too far from the truth. As she put away the perishable items, she promised herself that she would tip him generously the next time she had groceries delivered. Hopefully there would be a next time.

"How's it going?" She poked her head into the bathroom, suppressing the urge to laugh when she saw that Joseph was speckled and streaked with aqua-blue paint.

"I got kind of messy," he said. "But I haven't gotten any on the floor or the toilet or anything."

"And look how much you got done. Almost the whole wall, except for the top section. And the biggest wall, too. Nice work."

Just as she was helping Joseph to clean up outside, a panel truck pulled up with the items she'd purchased from the secondhand shop. She directed the two men through the messy space, watching as they set the pieces into place and even talked them into taking some of the old pieces out to the driveway. Like the grocery boy, they seemed to feel sorry for her living conditions, too, but they didn't refuse a tip.

She returned to the bathroom, picking up where Joseph had left off, and like him, she discovered it was rather fun to paint. Watching something old and messy transformed into something fresh and clean was invigorating. And the aqua-blue color was fresh and fun.

"That looks good, Mom." Joseph poked his head through the doorway.

"Thanks to your hard work."

"I moved my boxes to my room," he told her. "I haven't unpacked too much yet, but Danny wants me to play with him."

"Good idea." She felt relieved to think Joseph might have some fun.

By the time she finished cleaning up the messy paint things, it was getting dusky. Hopefully she'd have enough time to unpack some boxes, locate some kitchen pans and tools, and fix them some dinner before it was time to go up-stairs to watch her niece and nephew. She was just unpacking her dishes when she heard footsteps clomping down the steep wooden staircase and Joseph calling. "Aunt Marjorie asked if you want to help fix dinner," he explained. "That way she can get dressed." He frowned. "Except that she's *already* dressed."

"Oh, she means *dressed up*. She and Rich are going out tonight. I offered to babysit Danny and Lulu."

As she finished cleaning Marjorie's kitchen, Caroline couldn't remember the last time she'd felt this tired. Besides all the work in the apartment, she'd fixed the kids dinner, given Lulu a bath and put her to bed, played Chinese checkers with Joseph and Danny, and gotten Danny headed for bed (with

Joseph's help). Now it was only half past eight, but she was exhausted.

"I read Danny *two* picture books," Joseph said as he joined her in the kitchen. "And I told him if he didn't go to sleep without a peep, I wouldn't read him any books tomorrow. And he was quiet as a mouse."

"You're amazing." She ruffled his hair.

He shrugged. "Not really."

"Yes, you are," she insisted. "What would I do without you?"

"Be lonely?" He grinned.

She pointed to the kitchen clock. "And now it's time for you to start thinking about bed yourself, young man."

"Can I open my boxes from home first?" he asked. "I want to find some of my own books. I'm tired of reading baby books."

She laughed. "Yes, by all means find your own books. And I've got just the thing for you to store them on. As well as some of your other things. Tell you what, you stay up here to listen for the kids and I'll run down there and put it in your room."

It didn't take long to move the small pine bookshelf into Joseph's room. She placed it beneath the window, then stood back to look. With the bedside table and small dresser and desk, delivered earlier, this tiny space was looking more like a boy's bedroom. And instead of the additional furnishings making it look smaller, it almost seemed bigger. As she went upstairs, she felt invigorated again, suddenly eager to put more things in place. Except that she was babysitting and it seemed irresponsible to be that far from Danny and Lulu. But then she got an idea.

Joseph was thrilled at the idea of staying up late. And before long, dressed in his pajamas and robe and armed with some "big boy" books, he took his post in the living room and she went down to the apartment to continue putting their new home into order. "I'll leave the door open," she called. "Come and get me if you need anything."

As she unpacked boxes, she felt surprised at how many household items she really had. And she didn't miss the irony—realizing that her kitchen cupboards were packed full, meanwhile Marjorie's were fairly sparse. But then Caroline and Joe had gotten married many years ago. She still had their treasured wedding gifts, as well as other things she'd accumulated over the years. And, of course, this kitchen was about one-fourth the size of the one upstairs. Still, it felt good to see a well-stocked kitchen.

Eventually it was past eleven and she knew it was high time Joseph went to bed. She went upstairs to find him curled up on the sofa with a book. She bent down to kiss him on the head, noticing a small splotch of aqua-blue paint still in his hair. "Thank you, my prince," she said quietly. "Now it's time for you to go to bed."

He nodded sleepily, starting to gather his things.

"Just leave it," she insisted. "I'll bring them down."

After he left, she picked up one of the books. It was one that had belonged to her as a child, one of her favorites—*The Wonderful Wizard of Oz*. As much as she'd enjoyed the movie and the memory of how she and Joe had taken little Joseph to see it, she still felt the book was better. She opened the first page and started to read, but just like the Cowardly Lion in the poppy field, she found her eyelids growing very heavy... feeling herself drifting off to sleep. Instead of dreaming about the Tin Man or the Scarecrow, she dreamed she was a car mechanic struggling to fix a long yellow convertible that belonged to the handsome stranger from the coffee shop.

Chapter 5

On Sunday morning, after fixing Joseph pancakes
for breakfast, Caroline went upstairs to see what time Marjorie and Rich were going to church and if it would be all
right to join them. "Oh, we weren't planning on going today," Marjorie told her. "We got home so late last night.
And I figured you'd be tired, too." She made an impish grin.
"Don't tell Mom and Dad, but we don't go *every* Sunday."

"Oh...okay." Caroline nodded.

"I'm hungry, Mommy." Danny tugged on Marjorie's bathrobe.

"Want to join us for breakfast?" Marjorie removed the baby
bottle from the hot water, giving it a shake. "I haven't got
anything started yet, but—"

"Thanks anyway," Caroline said quickly. "We already ate.
And I've almost got the kitchen set up so we should be all
right from here on out." She ran her hand over Danny's head.

"I want to respect your space, Marjorie. I think in the long run we'll be better off for it."

"Oh, yeah, sure." Marjorie frowned slightly as she handed Danny the bottle. "Go give this to your sister and I'll see what I can round up for your breakfast."

Caroline excused herself, then went back down to the apartment. "Looks like no church today," she told Joseph. "Unless we want to go on our own, but I don't even know where the church is."

"I saw a church when Uncle Rich brought us home that night," he told her.

"Near here?"

"I think so. It looked like a big box, and the windows were all lit up with colors."

"Do you think you could find this church?"

"Sure."

Caroline looked at the clock she'd hung in the kitchen last night. It was one that she and Joe had picked out together when Joseph was little. The friendly black cat, with eyes and tail that twitched back and forth with seconds, never failed to humor her. And if the cat's time was correct, it seemed reasonable that they'd be in time for a service.

"Okay." Caroline reached for her black handbag. "Let's see what we can find."

Joseph seemed to know which way to go and Caroline decided to just let him lead the way. It was a bright, pleasant morning, and, at the least, they would have an enjoyable stroll. However, she regretted her navy-blue suit. Made of wool, it was far too warm for these summery temperatures. She considered removing the jacket, but that seemed too informal for a Sunday service.

"Do you think it's much farther?" she asked Joseph after

about ten minutes. Of course, he didn't know. And just when she was about to give up, there, sure enough, was a square brick church with big stained-glass windows. "You're good," Caroline told him as they tentatively approached the stalwart building. The large sign in front gave the service schedule, but according to her watch, they were late for the first service. "Maybe we should come back—"

"Hello, hello," a stout elderly woman warmly greeted them. Wearing a purple dress and matching hat, she had a Bible under one arm and a big red handbag looped over the other. "Are you here for first service?"

"Well, yes, but—"

"No time to waste." The woman hooked her arm in Caroline's, leading them up the concrete steps. "I'm Mrs. Franklin, and I can tell you're new because I've never seen you before. And I know everyone in this church. My father helped build this church in 1878."

"I'm Mrs. Clark," Caroline said, "and this is Joseph."

"Pleasure to meet you, Mrs. Clark. Now you will take the first door to your right," Mrs. Franklin instructed. "And I will escort this handsome young man to Sunday school. Let me guess, are you in the fourth grade?"

"Third."

"Tall for your age, aren't you?"

"But I—" Caroline looked at Joseph, but he seemed unconcerned. "See you later," she called as Mrs. Franklin swooshed him away. Caroline stared at the big wooden door, which she assumed led to the sanctuary since she could hear the strains of a pipe organ coming through it. She had always disliked being late to church back home, but it felt even worse to come late to a church she'd never attended before. Taking in a deep breath, she gently pushed open the door and was met by a thin gray-haired man.

"Right this way, miss." He smiled as he led her down the aisle, clear to the middle, where he motioned to the pew on her right.

Fortunately, the congregation was singing a hymn, so her entrance wasn't quite as intrusive as she feared. The woman next to her handed Caroline a hymnal, even helped her to find the right page. As she joined in the singing of the familiar chorus, Caroline began to relax.

When the congregation sat down, Caroline attempted to gather her bearings. Although this church wasn't the same denomination as she was accustomed to, it felt familiar and she suspected it was similar. The reverend was well spoken and intelligent, and his message was from the scriptures. Perhaps Joseph had found them a good church after all.

As she scanned the backs of the congregation, she felt slightly surprised to see that the women here, like Mrs. Franklin, appeared to enjoy wearing bright-colored clothing. So much so that Caroline felt rather dowdy and dark in her somber navy suit.

As the benediction was given, Caroline took a moment to study the stained-glass windows on both sides of the sanctuary. The one to her left showed three crosses on a green hillside, with light beams and a rainbow behind it. But when she looked at the one on her right, she nearly gasped at its beauty. It must've been facing east since the sun was pouring through it. She stared in awe and wonder, taking in the amazing depiction of a ten-foot-tall shepherd holding a lamb in his arms, surrounded by green pastures and sapphire-blue streams. She could hardly take her eyes off it.

She realized the service had ended while she was still staring at the shepherd image when the woman to her right gently nudged her. "It is lovely, isn't it?"

Caroline blinked and nodded. "I'm sorry. You probably wanted out."

"No hurry." The older woman stuck out a gloved hand. "I'm Mrs. Pruitt."

Caroline introduced herself, gathered her purse, and stood up, moving out of the way so the others in the pew could make their exit. But instead of leaving with them, Caroline remained behind, slipping into an empty pew in order to simply stare at the window...to absorb its beauty. Surely, no one would mind.

"I see we meet again," a vaguely familiar male voice said from behind her.

She turned around to see the stranger from the coffee shop smiling in amusement at her. At first she thought she was imagining things, and for a brief moment she wondered if this was part of last night's dream. Did he have a yellow convertible for her to repair?

Determined to remain poised, she smiled politely. "I was just admiring this gorgeous window." She turned her attention back to the glowing glass.

"It is beautiful. Especially this time of day. And this time of year the light angle is perfect. It really makes the color come alive. There are seventeen different shades of green in that window, and nearly that much of the blue tones, too."

"Spoken like an artist." She peered curiously at him. "Or at least someone with an appreciation for art."

He nodded with a thoughtful expression. "I've always loved looking at it."

"Oh, there you are, Terry." A strikingly attractive blond woman hurried toward them. Dressed in a pale pink linen suit and pearls, she looked like a cover girl for *Vogue* magazine. Or maybe a film star. "The Buckaroos are waiting for you. I promised them I'd round you up." She glanced curiously at Caroline. "Sorry to steal him from you, but believe me, those young men can get impatient. I was getting worried that they were getting ready to string me up." She smiled as she stuck out her hand to Caroline. "I'm Evelyn Stuart. I don't believe we've met."

"I'm Caroline Clark." She nervously shook the woman's hand. "Please, don't let me keep you."

"Yes. Thanks. Come on, Terry," Evelyn urged. "The natives are restless."

"Excuse me," he said as Evelyn tugged him away.

Not wanting to appear as if she was following them, Caroline remained put. As she stared up at the window, she wondered that this Terry person didn't introduce himself, but then he'd hardly had the chance when Evelyn had pulled him off like that. Caroline studied the window. Did it really have seventeen shades of green? No matter, it would be just as pretty with sixteen. Although it didn't seem quite as breathtaking as it had before. Maybe the sunlight had shifted or a cloud had dimmed the light.

"Mom?"

Caroline turned to see Joseph coming toward her. For some reason she felt extremely delighted to see him. Her little man! "Oh, there you are," she said as she embraced him, holding him tightly.

"Are you okay?" he asked when she finally let him go.

She smiled down at him. "I'm perfectly fine." She gestured to the window. "I was just enjoying the view in here. You were absolutely right, the windows here are very pretty."

He looked up and nodded, and for a long moment they both just stood there gazing at it.

"Did you enjoy Sunday school?" she asked as they started to leave the sanctuary.

"I wasn't sure at first, but then I decided I did like it."

"Good." She paused in the foyer, trying to remember which was the way out.

"Can I become a Buckaroo?" he asked.

"What exactly is a Buckaroo?"

"It's kind of like Boy Scouts, but it's part of this church. First off, you have to be a boy, and you got to be at least ten years old, and have your parents' permission."

"But you're not ten yet." She tried the biggest door, giving it a push; she saw daylight outside. She was eager to be back in the sunshine... to regain her balance.

"I'm *almost* ten," he reminded her as he helped pull open the heavy door. "It won't be long until I'm ten."

"Then maybe you should ask me about the Buckaroos in early February." She put her arm around his shoulders as they went down the exterior steps. "It'll be here before you know it."

"Then can we come back here next Sunday?" he asked eagerly.

"You really want to?"

"Yeah!" He nodded eagerly. "I made a friend. Jimmy Rolland. And he told me I'll go to the same school as him."

"How does Jimmy Rolland know that?"

"'Cause I told him where we live. Well, not exactly, because I don't know our new address exactly. But I told him the street name and stuff. And he said I will probably go to McKinley Elementary just like him. And he said school starts up on Wednesday, the day after New Year's Day."

"That's actually correct. All of it."

"See, I told you Jimmy knew."

"Jimmy sounds like a smart boy."

"And he doesn't live very far away from Aunt Marjorie's," Joseph continued.

"That's convenient." As they walked, she couldn't stop thinking about the stranger named Terry. At least that's what she thought Evelyn had called him. "Do you know who leads the Buckaroos?" Caroline asked a bit timidly as they came up to their apartment.

"Jimmy said his name is Terry. But not like a girl Terry. A guy Terry."

"Uh-huh." She removed her hat, pausing to study its very conservative design. It looked like something an old lady would wear. But for some reason she hadn't cared before.

"And Jimmy said he's going to call me *Joe*." Joseph paused to look at her. "Is that okay? I mean if Jimmy calls me Joe?"

She smiled down at him. "That's completely up to you, dear."

"I know that was Dad's name. You called him Joe, and you called me Joseph so you wouldn't mix us up. But since Dad's . . . well, gone, you wouldn't mix us up anymore."

Caroline felt a lump in her throat as she leaned down to hug her son. "You're right. I wouldn't mix you up, Joseph. But you are very much like your dad. And for that I am thankful."

He hugged her back, then looked earnestly into her eyes. "So, if it's okay, I'll be Joe now. And when I go to my new school, everyone will call me Joe Clark. *Okay?*"

She nodded. "Yes, that's fine." She removed her jacket. "But you'll have to be patient with me if I forget and still call you Joseph sometimes."

"Oh, that's okay. Moms can do that."

"Hello down there?" Rich's voice called from up above. "Anybody home?"

"We're here," Joseph called brightly as he dashed up the stairs. No, not Joseph anymore—except for her and only if she forgot—but *Joe*. Just like his dad. Just Joe. Joe Clark. Yes, it sounded right for a young man. And yes, she thought she could remember that, too.

"Uncle Rich wants to take me and Danny to the park," Joe announced when he returned. "Can I go?"

"Of course." And she didn't even bother to tell him to change out of his church clothes first, because he was already peeling them off as he sprinted to his bedroom.

As she changed back into her dungarees and work shirt, she felt like she had made the right decision coming here. Joseph—make that *Joe*—seemed happy. He seemed like he was already making a good adjustment. He'd made a friend and was eager about school. Now if only she could find a job... a way to keep him here.

To distract herself from fretting over her employment prospects, she rolled up her sleeves and went to work unpacking the rest of her boxes, putting things in place, and even using the leftover yellow paint to paint the few small walls of the kitchen. The black cat clock would look much sharper against the lemon-yellow paint color. Seeing that it was nearly two, she figured it was a good time to stop. Rich would probably be back with the boys soon.

She was just in the side yard, cleaning the yellow paint out of the paintbrush, when Marjorie came around the corner. "There you are, Sis."

"Hi, Marjorie." Caroline stood up straight, smiling at her sister. She looked sweet in a blue-and-white-striped dress. "You look as fresh as a daisy!"

"And you look like a mess."

"Thanks."

"Sorry." Marjorie patted her midsection. "I just wanted to wear this dress once more before I got too big for it. Looks like you've been painting."

"I have. Thanks so much for that leftover paint. It was perfect."

"Oh, good." Marjorie patted a yawn. "I was about to lie down, but Rich called."

"Oh, no, is something wrong?"

"Not at all. He and the boys were having such a grand time, he decided to take them to the beach."

"To the beach?" Caroline felt worried.

"Rich said that Joseph really wanted to see the ocean, and they weren't that far away. And it's such an incredibly nice day. Believe it or not, our December weather isn't always like this. And it probably won't last long, either. Anyway, Rich was excited to see Joseph's face when he saw the ocean for the first time."

Caroline wanted to say she would've enjoyed that, too, but simply dropped the clean paintbrush down to the grass to dry. "Well, that was very nice of Rich. I appreciate it. I know Joe—that's what he wants to be called now, Joe, not Joseph—anyway, he must be over the moon."

"And the best news is that they probably won't be home until dinnertime. Oh, yeah, Rich got the boys hot dogs. And he told me, Danny said he would take a nap on the beach." She laughed. "I'll just bet he will."

"Well, at least he'll be tired when he gets home. You can give him a bath and put him to bed."

"Sounds lovely. And now, while Lulu's napping, I shall catch some winks myself. We had such a great time last night. Stayed out too late. But you only live once, right?"

Caroline wiped her hands on the back of her dungarees.

"And I want to come down and see whether my sister is a good painter," Marjorie called over her shoulder as she walked away.

"Anytime," Caroline called back.

As she went back inside the apartment, she realized that the boys' beach trip was benefiting her with more time to finish things up. If she worked fast, who knew how much she could get done. Her friends who were full-time housewives sometimes marveled at what Caroline was able to accomplish. Caroline never said as much, but she attributed it to being a career woman. You learned to make every minute count.

She pulled out the upholstery fabric she'd fallen in love with yesterday. It was a pleasant print in clean shades of yellow, green, and aqua blue. She had planned to use it for a slipcover for the sad, worn sofa and perhaps some curtains for the small window on the front wall. On closer inspection of the sofa, she realized that she could create a slipcover simply by cutting, wrapping, and tucking the fabric. As a result, she was able to camouflage the unattractive piece with very little sewing. But while she had her sewing machine out, she whipped up a pair of curtains as well. They weren't fancy, but the colors were cheery, and the privacy was welcome. Now she unrolled the large braided rug she'd found at the secondhand store yesterday. It was mostly shades of green . . . and that made her stop and think of what Terry had said about the stained-glass window. *Seventeen shades of green.*

Not that she wanted to think about him. Although it was hard not to. Because really, what were the chances of meeting the same attractive man two days in a row like that? As well as having a conversation? What could it possibly mean? Probably nothing! For all she knew the lovely Evelyn was Terry's wife. And they both appeared to be in their mid-thirties, which usually meant married. And even if they weren't married, what difference did it make? Caroline was not looking for a man. Like she always told everyone, she was content to be single for the rest of her days. No one could replace Joe. Besides, she had little Joe to think of. And she needed to remain focused on him, providing for him.

By four o'clock, she was tweaking and moving things. Playing house. She added a couple of new throw pillows she'd found on sale yesterday. Covered in a spring-green-checked fabric, they looked fabulous with the new slipcover on the sofa. She pulled out the afghan she'd crocheted during the war, draping it over the back of the old rocker that had come with the apartment. Its stripes of varying shades of green seemed to add life to the old chair. She dug out the few pictures she'd brought with her, hanging them on some existing nails until she located a hammer. Then she played with the secondhand-store lamps, trying them out everywhere until she set the floor lamp by the rocker and the table lamp on the end table by the sofa. Perfect.

When she finally finished, the place looked pretty good—bright and clean and cheery. She'd even hung her favorite yellow towels in the bathroom, admiring the color contrast against the aqua blue. And she'd laid down the colorful rag rug her mother had given her a few years ago. The room looked clean and bright now—her son would no longer need to be fearful in here.

She took a quick shower; then, as she laid out some things for their dinner, she turned on the radio she'd set on top of the refrigerator. It was the same set she and Joe had purchased during the first year of their marriage. She turned the tuner until she heard the familiar sweet strains of the Glenn Miller Orchestra playing "Little Brown Jug." She knew that Glen Miller, like her Joe, had not made it home, but for a refreshing change, his music did not make her sad tonight. Instead, she felt surprisingly lighthearted as she lit the gas flame beneath her old copper teakettle and got out the makings for tea. Home sweet home.

Chapter 6

"Yoo-hoo?" Marjorie's voice called down the stairs just as the kettle started to whistle. "Anybody home?"

"Hello," Caroline called back. She glanced at the cat clock to see it was a bit after five now. "Is Rich back yet?"

"Not yet," Marjorie answered. "Can Lulu and I come down to see your painting progress?"

"Yes, of course." Caroline ran to meet her. "Here, let me take Lulu for you. These stairs are steep. Be careful."

"Thanks." Marjorie surrendered the baby. "I really do hate these steps. Rich had talked about changing them, but we've been so busy. To be honest, Rich has been feeling guilty about putting you and Joseph—I mean Joe—down here. He'd hoped to have more than just the bedrooms cleaned, but—*what on earth*?" Marjorie stood at the bottom of the steps just staring with a shocked expression. "Are you kidding me?"

Caroline couldn't help but laugh. "It looks a little better, eh?"

"Did you do this? All by yourself?" Marjorie went over to

the bright sofa, picking up a pillow and examining it. "This is really pretty."

"I found those at Fuller's Department Store yesterday," Caroline explained. "Marked down for their year-end sale."

"I can't believe you did all this." Marjorie continued walking around, studying everything and commenting in disbelief. *"How did you do all this?"*

"With a little planning and a lot of hard work." Caroline set Lulu down while she filled her teapot with hot water. "Care for a cup of tea?"

"This is just amazing." Marjorie peeked into the bathroom. "Truly amazing!"

"Joe helped me paint that room."

"But it's all so clean and orderly and pretty." Marjorie returned to the little kitchen area, picking up Lulu. "Did you know your auntie is a miracle worker?" she said to Lulu.

Caroline set the rooster teapot and matching cups and saucers on the table, then returned with a small plate of wafer cookies. "Sorry I didn't have time to bake." She giggled.

"I am just stunned." Marjorie continued looking around the room as she sat in the kitchen chair. "Utterly stunned."

"Oh, it wasn't that hard." Caroline quickly described some of the things she'd done, trying to play down how much work it had been or how she'd stayed up late last night after Marjorie and Rich got home, working on it.

"But you did all this in less than three days. I have been in my new house for a month now and it doesn't look nearly as nice as this."

"Of course, it does." Caroline poured their tea as Marjorie broke a cookie in half for Lulu. "Besides that, you've had your hands full with two little ones. I honestly don't know how you managed to paint those rooms with—"

"Rich's mother watched the kids for me. For almost two weeks. And the most I accomplished was to paint two rooms. Rich's dad did all the rest of the painting." Marjorie looked somewhat upset.

"But you sewed curtains and—"

"But there's so much *more* to do. Our house looks so bare and boring compared to this, Caroline. It's not fair."

Caroline laughed as she reached for a cookie. "Your house is about six times bigger than this. It should take at least six times longer to fill it up."

"But everywhere I look—it's just so perfect. Everything looks like it belongs together. It's so warm and inviting. My house will never look like this."

"Don't forget that Joe and I were married more than ten years ago. I've still got our wedding gifts, and over the years I've collected other household items. Give yourself time, Margie."

Marjorie let out a sad sigh. "I don't want Rich to see this," she said quietly. "He'll think that I've been lazy."

Caroline laughed heartily at this. "I seriously doubt that. Chasing after two little ones, pregnant with the third, I don't think that's exactly lazy."

"You should get married again," Marjorie said suddenly.

"Married?" Caroline set her cup down. "Where did that come from?"

"Well, look at how domestic you are. I mean, here I've always thought of you as this career girl, but you have a very domestic side to you, too. You would make someone a good wife."

Caroline chuckled. "Perhaps I think there is more to life than being a good wife."

"But you're *thirty-one*," Marjorie reminded her. "If you don't get married soon, you'll be too old to have more children. And think about it—if you hurried up and got married, you could have a baby not too long after I have mine. The cousins could play together and—"

"Oh, Marjorie." Caroline tried to hide her exasperation. "I'm sorry to disappoint you, but I really have little interest in marrying again."

"Why?"

"Why...?" Caroline got an unwanted image of Terry just then.

"Yes," Marjorie insisted, *"why?"*

Caroline twisted her wedding band, trying to think of a logical answer.

"And why are you still wearing that?" Marjorie demanded. "Good grief, you might as well hang a sign around your neck that says 'unavailable' as to go around with your wedding ring on. Really, Caroline. *Why?*"

With a cookie-smeared face, Lulu clapped her hands together, then pointed to the cookie plate, and Marjorie gave her a whole cookie. As the little cherub happily bit into it, Caroline felt her argument against remarriage growing weaker. The truth was, she would love to have a little girl like Lulu. What woman wouldn't? She looked down at her ring. "I wear this ring because it reminds me of Joe," she said softly.

"You think you would forget Joe if you took it off?"

"No, of course, not. I'll never forget Joe."

"What do you think Joe would want for you?"

Caroline pressed her lips together. She knew exactly what he wanted. They had talked about it before he'd gone off to war.

"What would he want for you, Caroline?"

"Joe would want me to be happy," she answered.

"And never marry again?"

"No, of course not. If you must know, Joe told me that if he didn't make it back, he wanted me to marry again."

"Aha!" Marjorie shook her finger at her. "And you didn't do it."

"There was no one around...I mean no one I felt like marrying. And, besides, I know that Joe told me that because little Joseph was so young. He didn't want me to bring him up alone. He said he would need a father. But now Joe's almost ten and—"

"Are you saying Joe doesn't need a father *now?*"

"At least he's got an uncle." Caroline looked up at the cat clock. "Speaking of that, shouldn't they be home by now?"

"Yes. And I should be getting dinner ready. Are you and Joe joining us?"

Caroline pointed to the kitchen counter where she'd set ingredients for spaghetti. "I thought I'd cook our dinner down here. We can't keep imposing."

Marjorie looked slightly disappointed. "Well, maybe it's for the best. I think I'll just fix something fast and easy and get Danny to bed. I'm sure he'll be grouchy as a bear."

"Speaking of the bear." Caroline leaned her head to one side. "I think I hear a car in the driveway."

Marjorie stood with Lulu. "Thanks for tea. And don't think we're done with the remarrying conversation, Sis. Really, it's high time you took off that wedding ring."

On Monday morning, Caroline donned a serious-looking suit and went upstairs to ask Marjorie if she minded having Joe for the morning. "I want to put in applications around town, and although I could take Joe with me, it might not look very professional. Plus I'm sure he'd be terribly bored."

"Joe is welcome here anytime." Marjorie rinsed a dish. "And since Danny doesn't have preschool and has ants in his pants today, Joe is doubly welcome."

As if on cue, Danny grabbed Joe's hand. "Come on, buddy, let's go play outside. Okay, Mommy?"

"Okay by me."

"You be a good helper for Aunt Marjorie." Caroline blew Joe a kiss as his little cousin tugged him out the back door.

Marjorie set the dish in the drainer, then turned to Caroline. "And you're going to apply at MG Chocolates, right? Rich told me to be sure and remind you to go there. Those assembly line jobs will probably fill quickly."

"Yes, I'm definitely going there. But I want to stop by some other businesses, too. If I could find a secretarial job, well, I think it would be better than the assembly line...in the long run. Although I'm willing to do whatever it takes to support Joe and me."

"Good luck." Marjorie shook her head as she dried her hands. "Although I have to say you look pretty old-fashioned in that outdated suit. Let me guess—you've had it since before the war began. You altered it during the war and then again afterward."

She looked down at her somber charcoal-colored suit. "Well, I—"

"And, no offense, but wearing your hair like that makes you look like an old schoolmarm."

Caroline reached up to touch her tightly pinned hair. "I just want to be taken seriously."

"I know, but this is California, Sis. The style out here is more easygoing and youthful, you know? Women pay more attention to fashion. Especially since the war ended." She touched her own shoulder-length hair. "Women have been letting their hair down and wearing colorful clothes. And some of us even use lipstick."

Caroline nodded. "Yes, I sort of gathered that at church yesterday."

"You went to church?"

Caroline quickly explained about Joe directing their way to church.

Marjorie grabbed Caroline's left hand, staring at her bare ring finger. "At least you've done one thing right."

Caroline made a sheepish smile. "I thought about what you said. It made sense." She didn't confess that it had been a tearful moment when she'd removed the ring last night, or that she felt uneasy and vulnerable without it today. "It will probably help when I'm applying for a job. Most businesses feel better about hiring single women."

"Good for you. And I suppose we can address your wardrobe issues later."

Caroline just sighed.

"In fact, I think I'm getting a plan." Marjorie made an impish smile. "A really good plan."

"Oh, dear!" She made a mock-horrified face.

"Yes!" Marjorie clapped her hands like Lulu. "A perfect plan!"

"What?"

"I'll tell you more when you come home."

"I can hardly wait," Caroline said dryly. "Anyway, I doubt I'll be gone long. I should be back by noon."

"No worries if you're not. Joe is just fine here."

Caroline told her goodbye, then, feeling a bit like a girl heading out for her first day of school, she walked toward town. As she walked, she prayed a silent prayer, asking God to help her find the right job. And then, since Rich had been so helpful and since he'd even asked Marjorie to remind her, she decided to go to the chocolate factory first. Get it out of the way. The truth was she did *not* want to work the assembly line, but she knew she couldn't afford to turn her nose up at anything. Besides, it wasn't as if they were going to offer her a job today.

As she turned onto Main Street, she remembered that Terry Whatever-His-Last-Name-Was worked in the chocolate factory. Certainly this wasn't the first time this had occurred to her, but it wasn't a comforting thought. Something about the man made her feel off balance, and the idea of running into him was unsettling. She suspected he worked in sales. Attractive guys like him almost always worked in sales. And although they were smooth talkers and not hard on the eyes, she had learned over the years that they were not always to be trusted. She didn't like being judgmental and would never say this to anyone, but she'd found that many of them were disingenuous.

As she came to the big brick building, she paused under the striped awnings of the chocolate shop, gazing into the plate glass window, where all sorts of beautiful chocolates were displayed. Just looking at them made her mouth water.

As she pushed open the big glass door that led into the marble-tiled foyer of MG Chocolates, the first thing that hit her was the aroma—the sweet, heady smell of chocolate nearly swept her off her feet. Had these people considered bottling this scent and selling it as perfume? Next she noticed a large display case filled with colorful candy boxes, stacked in a decorative way. Very pretty.

The sound of a jangling phone reminded her why she was here. And suddenly she felt nervous. But then she reminded herself that she had been a loyal and dependable employee for a total of nearly ten years. She had much to offer. Even if it was on an assembly line. She braced herself, standing up straighter.

"May I help you?" a pretty redheaded woman asked brightly.

"I would like to apply for a job," Caroline said politely. "My brother-in-law works here, and he suggested I come in this morning." Then, because the young woman seemed interested, she went on to tell her Rich's name and how her sister had lived in California since before the war and how Caroline had left a good secretarial job behind in Minnesota to live with them. "Sorry," she said quickly. "I didn't mean to go on and on. I suppose I'm a little nervous."

The woman smiled. "That's okay, I thought it was interesting. Let me call Mr. Stokes—he's our personnel manager—I think he might want to see you."

"Oh...thank you." She nodded, waiting as the woman spoke on the phone, and then, just like that, she was directed to go up the stairs and down the hallway to her right.

"Then turn right and it's the third door down," the woman told her. "It says *Personnel* on the door. Just knock and Mr. Stokes will call you in."

Caroline thanked her again and, feeling even more nervous, went up the stairs and down the hallway. She had expected to simply be handed an application, to fill it out, turn it in, and leave. But now it seemed she was about to meet the head of Personnel. Mr. Stokes. Hopefully his first name wasn't Terry. That might be awkward, but at least she would finally have a proper introduction.

She took in a steadying breath as she knocked. A deep voice said to come in, and she timidly opened the door. But to her relief it was a heavyset man with deep jowls and thinning gray hair. "Good morning," she said with as much confidence as she could muster. "My name is Caroline Clark, and I was told to come speak to you." She made an uneasy smile. "I came to MG Chocolates under the impression I would fill out an application for employment and leave it here. But the receptionist told me to—"

"You told Miss Warner that you worked as a *secretary*, correct?"

"Miss Warner?"

"Our receptionist. She was under the impression you had been employed as a secretary."

"Oh, yes, yes," she said eagerly. "I've worked in two different businesses as a secretary, for a total of nearly ten years. My training was from Miss Mayfield's Secretarial School, where I ranked in the top five percentile of my class. I worked at my last place of employment for almost five years. And I have several letters of recommendation right here with me." She patted her handbag.

He fumbled through a pile of papers then, finding his glasses, slipped them on, and peered curiously at her. "Please, take a seat, miss."

She sat down, feeling suddenly hopeful. "Do you have a secretarial position open?" she asked cautiously.

"Well, we didn't have one last week. But during this past weekend one of our secretaries went skiing." He scowled at her. "Do you ski?"

"I haven't in years."

"Good. Dangerous sport. Miss Bentley broke her leg. Now let me see those letters of recommendation."

She took the envelope containing copies of letters from her purse and handed them to him.

"Uh-huh..." He extracted the letters, taking his time to skim them. "Yes, this looks very good. Tell me a little about yourself, Miss Clark."

"Actually it's *Mrs.* Clark," she began. "But I'm widowed. My husband died early in the war." And then she talked about her secretarial training, the places she'd worked, and what she enjoyed most about working. "I'm very detail-oriented. I work quickly and efficiently. And I do everything I can to make my boss's job easier."

He laid down her letters and looked evenly at her without speaking, almost as if he was taking inventory. Then he asked her some specific questions about dictation, typing speed, and so on. "Well, if you're interested, you can have the job, Mrs. Clark."

"Thank you." She nodded eagerly. "What job would that be?"

"Mr. Glen Hancock is vice president of Production. His secretary, Miss Bentley, will be out for at least six weeks."

"So you're offering me *temporary* work?" Caroline felt her spirits dive.

"Well, you can look at it like that," he spoke slowly, "or you can look at it like the opportunity it is. MG Chocolates is the largest employer in this town, and we're growing fast. If you prove yourself a valuable employee, who knows what might come six weeks from now? Mr. Gordon appreciates motivated workers with good team spirit. From what I've read here and from what little time we've spent together, I suspect you could be just that sort of team player we're looking for, Mrs. Clark."

She brightened. "Yes! I am a team player. I really am."

"Then you'll accept the job?"

"Yes, of course. Gladly. Thank you very much, Mr. Stokes."

"Great." He handed her some official papers. "Fill these out right now, and I'll ask one of the girls to give you a tour of the facility." He grinned. "Oh, yes, I forgot to ask. You do like chocolate, don't you?"

"I *love* chocolate."

He nodded. "I thought so."

"The smell alone in this place has me slightly light-headed."

"I remember that, too..." He looked dismayed. "I'm sorry to say that it wears off over the years. Unless I've been on vacation, I usually walk in and hardly notice it."

"But you still like chocolate?" she asked.

"Oh, yes. Most assuredly." He patted his midsection. "It probably shows."

Caroline felt slightly giddy as she handed him back the paperwork. *She had a job!* Just like that—she had a job. It was almost too much to take in. As she watched him browsing over the completed forms, she realized they hadn't discussed her wage yet.

"I always feel a bit awkward speaking about salary and benefits and such," she explained a bit timidly. "But because I'm the breadwinner of our little family, it's a necessity."

"Little family?" He looked surprised.

"Oh, yes." She felt a stab of worry. "Didn't I mention I have a son?"

"No, you did not. May I ask who cares for your young son?"

"My son isn't so young. He's nearly ten years old and very mature for his age," she said defensively.

"Even so, children need watching. And sometimes they get sick. What happens then?"

"We live with my sister. She's a homemaker with two little ones. When Joe comes home from school, my sister will be there. And I'm sure she will be happy to help out if he should get sick. My mother used to do those things for me."

"Oh, well, then it seems you've got this all figured out." His smile returned.

It wasn't the first time she'd experienced this line of thinking. Many people in the workforce questioned the sensibility of working mothers. Like Marjorie, some acted as if it were her moral responsibility, as a mother, to find a replacement father for her son. As if it were that easy! Thankfully this was not going to prevent her from getting this job. As she signed the last form Mr. Stokes had for her, she felt relieved that she hadn't mentioned Joe to him earlier. That might've ruined everything. Once again, she inquired about her wages and, as he explained the salary structure and benefits, she was pleased to discover that she would be better off here than she had been in Minnesota!

Chapter 7

Caroline was sent back down to the redheaded receptionist, Miss Warner, for her tour of the facility. "First things first." Miss Warner opened a box of chocolates, holding it out to Caroline. "Just so you fully understand what we do here," she said with a smile. Then while Caroline sampled a delicious chocolate, Miss Warner made a phone call, and after a few minutes, a woman in a white uniform showed up.

"Betty works the assembly line, but fills in for me during breaks or if I'm giving a tour," Miss Warner explained as she led Caroline down a hallway. "We'll start at the beginning." Before long they were in a large warehouse area. "This is where the ingredients for chocolate are delivered and stored." She pointed to containers, explaining their contents. From there, they went to the actual manufacturing area, where enormous machines were noisily operating. Miss Warner led Caroline to a cordoned-off area, where they could observe the machinery and people at work. "This viewing section is where we bring groups during our tours. Much safer than being down on the floor."

"Do you give many tours?" Caroline asked loudly to be heard.

"Tours became so popular with the public that we scheduled them for Wednesday mornings. But if it's a client, we give them a private tour at any time, complete with full sampling privileges."

"Sampling must help with sales." Caroline was craving another chocolate.

"Most definitely." Miss Warner waved her hand to the large wide-open area that occupied the center of the building. "This is what we call Production and Packaging, and it's the part of the business that your boss, Mr. Hancock, is in charge of. As you can see, this is where the chocolates are made and boxed." She pointed out the various machines, explaining what they did, how much they produced, and so many details that Caroline felt slightly overwhelmed.

"Everything looks very modern and efficient." Caroline mentally compared it to the leather company, which besides being much older was much dirtier. "And everything looks so sanitary!" Even the assembly line workers appeared clean and tidy in their crisp white uniforms with red trim. And everyone had on neat white caps that completely covered their hair. Many of them wore white gloves as well.

"We produce a very high-quality product," Miss Warner said proudly.

Caroline nodded. "Very impressive."

Next Miss Warner took her to Distribution and Delivery, explaining the various ways orders were packaged and shipped. "Most of our chocolates are just stock orders—for larger stores. But we also do special orders for smaller stores. And then we do individual orders, too. Those are shipped by mail anywhere in the U.S." She pointed to a white and red delivery truck that was currently being loaded. "We run eight trucks now, but Mr. Gordon wants to work up to a dozen by the end of next year." She glanced at her watch. "Which reminds me—this is New Year's Eve and the factory will be closing early today, so I better keep us moving. I've still got a lot to do before three o'clock."

Miss Warner led her to an elevator in the front of the building. "I usually take the stairs," she said as she pushed the button. "The elevators are for executive personnel. But when we give client tours, I'm allowed to take this elevator. And, since you work for an executive, you get to use it, too."

As the doors closed, Caroline observed that the elevator, like the foyer, had a marble floor and handsomely carved wooden walls. Impressive.

"I think we'll skip the second floor," Miss Warner said as she pushed the button for the third floor. "Besides, you already saw some of it when you went to Mr. Stokes's office. The rest is mostly storage and a few offices for bookkeeping and finances—middle-management stuff."

On the third floor, Miss Warner showed Caroline a large employee lunchroom, which overlooked Production and Packaging down below. The sounds and smells of the chocolate production wafted up. She pointed out where employee lockers, restrooms, and even shower rooms were located. Everything was clean and practical, plain and utilitarian.

"Will I have a locker, too?" Caroline asked eagerly.

"No, this area isn't for you. I just wanted you to see it—to get the lay of the land."

"Oh..." Caroline wasn't sure what that meant as she followed Miss Warner back to the elevator. Was it because she was considered a temporary employee until Miss Bentley returned?

"Now we go up to the executive offices," Miss Warner said as she pushed the button for the fourth floor in the elevator. "There are four departments: Production, where you'll be working. Distribution, Marketing, and Sales. Each department has a vice president." Miss Warner started rattling off names, but Caroline knew she wasn't going to remember all this—she needed to take notes, and her fingers were itching for a steno pad.

As they exited the elevator, Caroline was immediately aware that they were on the executive floor. The foyer outside of the elevator, with marble floors and richly paneled walls as well as several handsomely potted plants, was even more posh and polished than the main entrance foyer downstairs. But what really captured her attention was the open walkway that appeared to circle the building. She peered over the brass rail to see that it overlooked the manufacturing floor, where her tour had started. It was four stories below them, but highly visible from this bird's-eye view.

"Some of the workers think the catwalk is so the VPs can spy on them," Miss Warner said quietly. "But I think it's just to make them feel connected."

"I like it," Caroline told her. "Makes for an interesting perspective."

"The offices on this side are for Production and Distribution. And over there, on the right side, are Marketing and Sales." Miss Warner pointed across the open area to the opposite end. "And that is the president's offices."

Miss Warner paused by a large glass door with the word *Distribution* in large letters. As they went inside, she introduced Caroline to a pleasant-faced young woman named Miss Fowler. Her blond hair was styled, and her gabardine suit was more fashionable than Caroline's.

"Our job in distribution is to get the product out of the

factory and to its final destination—in excellent condition," Miss Fowler told her. "It sounds simple enough, but believe me, it's not always easy." Then, as she was telling them about how a delivery truck broke down in a snowstorm up north, an older man stepped into the office. "And this is my boss, Mr. Price, vice president of Distribution." Miss Fowler quickly explained to him who Caroline was, and he said a polite but brisk hello, hurrying on into his office.

"Welcome to MG," Miss Fowler said cheerfully. "See you at lunch."

Caroline thanked her, and Miss Warner led her to the next glass door. "This is where you'll be working." Miss Warner pointed to the big gold letters, *Production*, as she led her into the spacious office area. Similar to the distribution office, this space was carpeted in a deep red rug, and several club chairs and a coffee table made a waiting area on one side and a large mahogany desk was on the other.

"That's Miss Bentley's desk," Miss Warner said, "but yours for now." She pointed to a door off to one side. "That's a closet for your things." She pointed to the opposite side. "And those are the offices of some of the production employees." Now she went over to the big door in the rear wall that said *Vice President of Production, Glen Hancock* in gold letters. "And that is your boss's office. Mr. Hancock." She gave the door three sharp knocks.

"Come in," a male voice called out.

Caroline felt nervous as she followed Miss Warner into the spacious office, where one whole wall was floor-to-ceiling windows. Everything about this place was so much bigger and grander than what she was used to at her previous place of work. She wondered if she was out of her league here. What if she couldn't measure up to their expectations?

"Good morning, Mr. Hancock," Miss Warner said respectfully. "I'd like you to meet your temporary secretary." She did a quick introduction. "Mrs. Clark will be filling in for Miss Bentley until she recovers from her broken leg."

Mr. Hancock stood and extended his hand. "Pleased to meet you, Mrs. Clark." He smiled warmly at her, but as she exchanged the usual pleasantries, she felt surprised that he wasn't older. Not that he was young, exactly, but her best guess was that he wasn't much more than forty. The VPs back at the leather factory had all been close to retirement age.

"I'm very impressed with the factory. Miss Warner just gave me the tour. And the machines and the automation all appear to be so very modern. Everything down there looks so sanitary and well organized. Very impressive." Caroline didn't want to blather, but she was trying to suppress her nerves.

"Great. Glad to see you appreciate a well-run factory. And I'm relieved they found someone so quickly." He sat back down at his desk and picked up a folder. "I was already starting to feel overwhelmed. Especially since Valentine's Day is only six weeks out. We're in our most demanding production season right now. I need someone who can jump right in where Miss Bentley left off."

"I'm ready to do that." Caroline hoped that was true, but she had her doubts. How ready was she really?

"So can you begin work *today?*" he asked hopefully.

"Well, I, uh, I don't know. I suppose I could."

"Tomorrow's a holiday," he reminded her. "And every day we lose in these next couple of weeks is critical."

"I'll start today," she declared. "I just need to give someone a call . . . let them know my plans."

"Thank you!" He nodded eagerly. "There's already quite a pile of correspondence on Miss Bentley's desk. Do what you can with it. And we close early today, so it will be a short day for you."

"I just want to finish her tour," Miss Warner said as they were leaving. "She hasn't seen the marketing and sales offices yet. Or Mr. Gordon's office."

"By all means, finish the tour." He waved them off. "And let me know if you have any questions, Mrs. Clark. I'm busy, but not too busy to help you get off to a good start."

"Yes, I'm sure I'll have some questions," she said as they backed out the door. "But I'll write them down so we don't waste too much of your valuable time."

"Good." He nodded. "I appreciate that."

Now Miss Warner led her in the opposite direction from the elevator. "This first office is the sales department." She peered in the door to what appeared to be an empty office. "But it looks like they might be in meetings. Mr. Russell is probably getting his salesmen ready for the big convention next week." Caroline vaguely wondered if this was where Terry worked. He'd seemed so smooth and polished . . . like a salesman.

Miss Warner led Caroline on down the catwalk, pointing to a large wooden door with no words on it. "This is the executive break room," she said as she pushed it open to reveal a surprisingly luxurious room—nothing like the break room Caroline had been acquainted with back in Minnesota. Besides a modern kitchen area, there were several glass-topped dining tables and a comfortable-looking seating area. Miss Warner made a longing sigh. "My dream is to be up here someday. Oh, I don't have the proper training yet, but I just started a secretarial correspondence course last fall. And sometimes I fill in for the middle-management secretaries, just for a few hours. Once I did a whole day. But they would never let me take six weeks."

"Well, good for you, for pursuing your dream." Caroline smiled.

Miss Warner paused in front of the next glass door. "And this is the lovely marketing department. Miss Stuart is the vice president of this department."

"Miss?" Caroline asked in surprise. "This vice president is a woman?"

"Yes." Miss Warner pushed open the door just as a fashionably dressed young woman emerged from the executive office. "Hello, Miss Thornton, this is Mrs. Clark. She will fill in for Miss Bentley."

Miss Thornton shook Caroline's hand with a questioning look. "Pleased to meet you, Mrs. Clark."

"Mrs. Clark just moved here from Minnesota," Miss Warner told her.

"Minnesota?" Miss Thornton's brow creased. "This must be quite a change for you."

"Yes, it takes some getting used to, but I'm happy to be here."

"So . . . welcome to the team," she said in a slightly superior way, "even if it's just *temporarily*."

"Thank you." Caroline noticed Miss Thornton narrowing her eyes ever so slightly, almost as if evaluating her. And judging by this secretary's stylish coral suit with its big shiny black buttons and her matching high-heeled pumps, she would probably concur with Marjorie—Caroline definitely looked dowdy and old-fashioned in comparison.

"Would you like to meet Miss Stuart now?" Miss Thornton offered. "I think she might be able to spare a minute or two."

"Yes," Caroline said, "I'd appreciate that."

Miss Thornton cracked open the door, calling out first. "Mr. Hancock's new secretary would like to meet you."

"I only have a minute, Barbara. Keep it short."

"Right this way." Miss Thornton led her in, jumping immediately into introductions, although this vice president seemed uninterested, keeping her back toward them as she studied what looked like an advertisement for chocolates.

Caroline stared openly at the back of the woman leaning against the large, elegant glass-topped desk. Wearing a sky-blue suit, with the poster in one hand and a cigarette in the other, she looked so chic that she might've been posing for her own advertisement. The caption would read: "The modern career woman at work today."

When Miss Stuart turned around, Caroline nearly fell over. It was the same blond woman she'd met in the sanctuary yesterday. The same gorgeous woman who had snatched Terry away from her. Caroline was speechless.

Evelyn appeared taken aback as well. She snuffed out her cigarette in a heavy glass ashtray, then approached Caroline with slightly narrowed eyes. "I believe we've already met."

"Yes." Caroline nodded nervously. "At church yesterday."

"Yes, that's right." Evelyn laid down the poster to shake Caroline's hand, staring at her with a skeptical expression.

"Well, isn't this nice," Miss Thornton said swiftly. "Everyone knows everyone now. So off we go, back to work, ladies, lots to do and not enough time to do it."

"That's right," Evelyn agreed. "Short day today."

Before they left the VP's office, Miss Warner pointed to Miss Thornton. "I'll bet *you* have big plans for New Year's Eve tonight."

"You've got that right." Miss Thornton smiled smugly as she slid into her desk chair, reaching for the phone. "Marketing," she said smoothly, "how can I help you?"

Caroline was still trying to get her bearings as they exited the office and walked around the catwalk. So Evelyn was Miss Stuart, not Mrs. That meant she and Terry weren't married. But did Terry really work here? She considered asking Miss Warner, but didn't want to appear overly interested.

"Those marketing ladies," Miss Warner said longingly. "If I had the right training, I'd love to work in that office."

"Why that office?" Caroline asked uneasily.

"Partly because they're so modern and stylish. But not only that. The marketing department is exciting. It's where all the fun happens."

"Fun?" Caroline wanted to remind Miss Warner this was a workplace, but didn't care to offend the young woman. Especially after she'd been so helpful and friendly.

"Oh, yeah. Everyone says that Miss Stuart gets away with murder around here."

"You mean because she's so pretty?" Caroline felt dismayed. Was this really *that* sort of company? She hadn't gotten that impression at all until now.

"I'm sure her looks don't hurt a bit. But it's also because she's so cozy with the boss. Her family and the Gordon family are really close. Have been for years. We've got a secret pool—some of us girls—where we try to pick the day when Mr. Gordon will propose to Miss Stuart. Some girls picked tonight—New Year's Eve. But I picked Valentine's Day."

"Uh-huh." Caroline didn't know what to think—but something about this was bothering her. "Isn't Mr. Gordon a bit old for Miss Stuart?"

"Oh, I don't know how old he is." She giggled. "Certainly, he's a lot older than me. And it's possible that all the speculation about him and Miss Stuart is wrong. I probably shouldn't repeat it."

"Maybe not." Caroline knew her tone came out chilly.

"Anyway, those marketing women really are fun," Miss Warner said a bit defensively. "Just wait, you'll see."

"Well, I must admit that Miss Stuart and Miss Thornton are quite glamorous, but I'm not sure I'd like to work in their office for that reason alone."

Miss Warner laughed. "Well, it's not for everyone." She pointed ahead. "One more stop. The big boss. Mr. Gordon might be a busy man, but he always wants to meet the new employees."

However, when they got to Mr. Gordon's very impressive executive suite, his secretary, a sweet older woman named Mrs. Gallagher, informed them he was on an important conference call. "I'm afraid he'll be on for another thirty minutes," she said. "But I'll let him know that Mr. Hancock has a replacement secretary. I'm sure he'll be relieved." She smiled warmly. "And welcome to the MG team, dear. I hope you like it here."

"And that completes your tour," Miss Warner informed Caroline when they were out on the catwalk again. "If you'll excuse me, I really should get back to the reception desk."

"Certainly. And thank you for the tour." Caroline frowned toward the executive suite, wondering if it were possible. But then slowly shook her head. Miss Warner had said Mr. Gordon was "a lot older."

"You can find your way back to your office from here okay?"

Caroline smiled at her. "No problem."

They parted ways at the elevator, and, feeling somewhat overwhelmed and a bit confused, Caroline returned to the production office. She put her handbag, hat, and gloves in the narrow closet, thinking how much nicer this was than a locker. But at the same time, she warned herself not to get used to it. She was over her head, and she knew it. If she could hold on for six weeks, she would be surprised.

Chapter 8

"Of course, you must stay and work," Marjorie assured Caroline after hearing the good news about the job. "Joe and Danny have been playing outside all morning. I tell you, Sis, your boy's a whiz at keeping Danny occupied. Maybe I should hire him as a babysitter."

"Joe always wanted a little brother. Danny is as close as he'll probably get." Caroline started sorting the large stack of mail with her free hand.

"Well, congratulations on getting a job so quickly. And such a good one, too. Rich will be happy to hear it."

"And because it's New Year's Eve, we quit early today, so I'll be home a little past three, and I can watch your kids tonight, in case you and Rich want to go out."

"No, we had our big date on Saturday. I just want a quiet evening at home."

"I should get to work." Caroline slit open an important-looking envelope.

"When you get home you can tell me all about it."

Caroline ended the call and continued sorting through the mail, separating the urgent from the mundane, and making a list of questions for her new boss. Then she went to work familiarizing herself with her new work space. But she quickly discovered that Miss Bentley (of the broken leg) was not nearly as organized as her tidy desktop had suggested. And if one dug a little, it was obvious that Miss Bentley's filing skills were "unique" at best. However, Caroline respected the fact that this was Miss Bentley's domain and her job was simply to fill in until she recovered.

Hopefully she would figure out the filing system and find a way to stay on task without changing too much. For now it seemed the most important job was to keep up with the mail, deal with Mr. Hancock's calls, take dictation as needed, transcribe the letters and orders that were ready to be sent out, and to keep everything in the production department moving as smoothly as possible.

Before long, she met two other production employees—Mr. Vincent, the production foreman, who split his time between the office and the floor, and Mr. Divers, the head mechanic in charge of keeping the machinery running smoothly. They spent nearly an hour meeting in Mr. Hancock's office before they broke up for lunch.

"Aren't you going to lunch?" Mr. Hancock asked as they were leaving.

She smiled as she put a receipt in the proper file. "I'll be right along." Of course, she had no intention of going to lunch today, but she didn't want her new boss to know. For one thing, she hadn't brought food with her, but besides that there was much to do, and three o'clock wasn't so far off that she couldn't wait. She planned to use the extra hour to get this space a bit more organized. And that meant moving a few things around—just temporarily, since she suspected Miss Bentley would probably want to go back to her old ways. But when Caroline returned on Wednesday, she wanted to hit the street running, as one of her old secretarial teachers used to say. Preparation was key to success.

After about twenty minutes of reorganizing, the big glass door swung open and Miss Fowler from the distribution department walked in. "What's going on in here?" she demanded with a scowl.

"Wh—what?" Caroline looked up from where she was kneeling by a file cabinet.

"It's the lunch hour, and here you are working." Miss Fowler's scowl melted. "You don't want to make the rest of us look bad. *Come to lunch!*"

Caroline stood with a sheepish smile. "The truth is I didn't bring a lunch today, so I thought I'd just work through. I didn't think anyone would mind."

"Don't you know that it's New Year's Eve? Mr. G always treats the entire company to a special lunch on special days. The folks downstairs get soup and sandwiches. But the executive employees get a catered lunch. And I must say today's selection isn't half bad." She smiled warmly. "Don't you remember I said I'd see you at lunch? I looked all around, but you weren't there."

"I didn't know about the catered lunch."

"Well, it's a tradition here. And if you want to partake, you better get moving."

Caroline closed the file drawer. "Then, of course, I'll come. Thank you, Miss Fowler."

"When we're off the clock, I'm just Doris," she said lightly.

"I'm Caroline."

"And since we work on the practical end of the company—Production and Distribution are considered the workhorses—we need to stick together."

"Thanks." Caroline gave her a grateful smile.

Doris seemed to be studying Caroline's suit as they walked down the catwalk. "So... is that how they dress back east, or wherever it is you're from?"

"Minnesota." Caroline shrugged. "This was an old suit that I remade for work a few years ago." She didn't admit to how many times she'd remade it. She frowned down at the dark gray woolen pieces. The ultraconservative design resembled a military uniform. "I suppose it does look like I'm going to a funeral."

"As long as it's not your own funeral." Doris laughed as she pushed open the break room door.

The room was bustling with people now. Besides the other secretaries, there were a number of men in suits, and everyone seemed to be in a festive mood. Some were standing in clumps and visiting, others were sitting at tables, but all of them appeared to have food and drink in hand.

"Check out this spread," Doris said as she led Caroline over to the buffet, which, though somewhat picked over, still had plenty of food. "I'm going to grab some of that chocolate cake, then I'll save you a place at my table."

Caroline picked up a plate and was just dishing out some Waldorf salad when someone got into the line behind her. She paused to see who it was, then clumsily dropped the serving spoon when she realized it was her mystery man—Terry. Apparently he really did work here after all. "I see we meet again." She tried to sound clever, but mostly felt awkward.

"What're *you* doing up here?" he asked with what seemed genuine surprise.

"As a matter of fact, I *work* here," she said lightly.

"Really?" He looked confused now. "You got hired on the assembly line?"

She chuckled. "Well, if that were the case, I wouldn't be up here now, would I? I'm sure I'd be tossed out on my ear."

He looked truly perplexed. "So, tell me, *where* do you work?"

"I was about to ask *you* the same thing." She put some asparagus spears on her plate.

"What?" He glanced around as if concerned that someone might be listening in.

"Oh, all right." She forked a slice of roast beef. "I suppose you haven't heard that Miss Bentley broke her leg skiing."

"Really?" He shook his head with a look of realization. "Poor Miss Bentley."

She lowered her voice now. "I came in to apply for a job this morning. Naturally, I assumed it would be on the assembly line, which I must admit was not terribly appealing. But then I was whisked off to Mr. Stokes's office. Well, I had no idea what was going on, so I just played along. The next thing I knew I was offered a job." She paused to ladle some gravy onto her serving of mashed potatoes. "Of course, it's only temporary, but I hear that Mr. Gordon likes team players and that this company is really expanding nicely, so perhaps if I play my cards right, well, you just never know." She smiled as she set the ladle back into the gravy. Terry was really a strikingly attractive man, and it was sweet the way he seemed to have taken an interest in her like this. "And now, you must tell me about your—"

"Mr. Gordon," Mr. Hancock called from across the room. "Glad to see you made it here. We heard you were running late."

"Thank you for the delicious meal," another VP said cheerfully. "And they say there is no such thing as a free lunch."

Everyone laughed heartily, and Caroline glanced around the room, trying to figure out which man was Mr. Gordon.

"You're all very welcome," Terry said loudly. "Happy New Year to everyone." Now he turned to Mr. Hancock, who was approaching them. "And I've just met your new replacement secretary. So sorry to hear about Miss Bentley. But it looks like you'll be in good hands."

"I certainly appreciate the speedy decision on the part of Mr. Stokes."

"That was fast, wasn't it?" Terry turned back around to the buffet, reaching for the roast beef.

"Mr. Gordon?" Caroline stammered. "You *are*...Mr. Gordon?"

"Yes." Terry smiled. "Pleased to meet you, uh, *Mrs.... ?*"

"Mrs. Clark." She set down her plate and nervously extended her hand.

"Ah, yes. *Mrs. Clark.*" He grasped it firmly. "Pleased to officially meet you. And welcome to the team."

"Thank you." As she made an uneasy smile, she felt her cheeks growing warm. How could she have been so stupid? Acting so smug, trying to be clever!

Evelyn sidled up to Mr. Gordon now. "I need to talk to you," she said in a slightly terse tone. "I left several messages with your secretary this morning, but you never returned my calls."

"I've been on the phone all morning." He continued to fill his plate.

"Well, I want to show you a new idea," she said urgently. "And I need you to see our revised Valentine ad campaign. I want it sent out by Wednesday and we need your approval by quitting time today—if that's not too much to ask."

"No problem. I'll stop by your office after lunch."

Caroline couldn't help but overhear their conversation as she gathered her silverware and studied the dessert selection.

"And I'm feeling unclear about something," Evelyn said a bit more quietly. "I thought we'd agreed that no executive staff would be hired without the exec team's approval."

Mr. Gordon glanced at Caroline as she put a piece of apple pie on a dessert plate. "I suppose you'll have to speak to Mr. Stokes about that."

"Really?" She sounded skeptical. "This was completely below your radar?"

"I only just learned of it myself," he said quietly.

"But the team decided that—"

"She's only a temporary replacement," he said in a quiet but firm voice. "I assure you, any full-time permanent employees will be approved in the future."

Feeling like an unwanted guest, Caroline slunk over to the table where Doris was waiting. "Have a seat." Doris lowered her voice. "And I see you met Mr. G. Isn't he a dish!"

Caroline gave her a tolerant smile and picked up her fork. Staring down at her food, she suddenly realized she'd lost her appetite. In fact, the pit of her stomach felt as if she'd already digested a rather large stone. She had never felt so foolish in her life. As she poked at her food, she tried to remember what she'd actually said to Mr. Gordon when she'd blathered away like that. Really, what on earth had she been thinking? Acting so glib and cheeky? So completely unprofessional.

It felt as if he'd gotten the last laugh, though. When he'd told Evelyn that Caroline was *only temporary*—it felt almost like getting a pink slip. And why not? After her stupid little act, he'd probably decided that she should be even more temporary than six weeks. Caroline wouldn't be the least bit surprised if they'd found a replacement for her by the time she returned to work on Wednesday. Oh, why on earth had she acted like that?

"Aren't you hungry?" Doris asked.

"I, uh, I guess not." Caroline glanced to the door, wondering if there was a graceful way to cut through the crowd and escape this room without making a further spectacle of herself.

She was about to stand when Mr. Gordon began to ding his fork on a water glass. "Excuse me, everyone," he said loudly. "I'd like to make a little announcement while you're all still here." He waited as the room grew quiet. "First of all, I want to thank you all for your hard work this past year. Although the year started out slowly, due to the war shortages and such, the last six months have surpassed all expectations. Thanks to everyone's efforts and our recent expansions and improvements, MG Chocolates has experienced its highest annual sales in the history of the company!" He paused while they all clapped with enthusiasm. "And now I want to wish each and every one of you a very happy and blessed new year." He held up his glass in a toast. "Here's to making 1946 even better than 1945."

"Hear, hear," everyone said heartily.

Mr. Gordon pointed to Evelyn now. "And I believe you have an announcement to make as well."

She smiled at everyone. "Mrs. Gordon and I have decided to combine our efforts for tonight's celebration. As some of you know, we were both hosting a New Year's Eve party this evening, and it was causing some controversy with our guest lists—some of you couldn't decide which party to attend." She laughed. "Therefore I have relocated my gathering to the gracious home of our founders, Mr. and Mrs. Gordon, and of course everyone here is invited."

"And my mother expects everyone to come, along with your wives or husbands or dates," Mr. Gordon told them. "Be there or be square."

They all laughed. Well, everyone except for Caroline. Despite her pasted-on smile, she felt like crying. But as the crowd grew loud and boisterous again, she saw her chance for a smooth getaway. Whispering to Doris that she felt unwell, she slunk around the backside of the buffet table, dumped the contents of her uneaten lunch in the kitchen area, then slipped out the door and back to the production department.

Sitting at Miss Bentley's desk, Caroline wondered if she should put everything that she'd just rearranged back into its former place. Just like she'd found it. But then she realized that her reorganization would actually make it easier for the returning secretary. Besides, she reminded herself as she started to transcribe a letter from Miss Bentley's steno pad, it was possible that she wasn't really about to be shown the door. Perhaps, if she minded her p's and q's, she might be able to keep this job until the end of the week.

As she continued working, finishing up some correspondence that Miss Bentley had left behind, pausing to answer the phone as needed, Caroline was determined to be so efficient and well mannered that Mr. Hancock would not want her to leave until her six weeks were up. After that, well, who knew?

When three o'clock finally came, she felt as if she'd put in a ten-hour day. She knew it was mostly due to the stress—stress she had brought on herself by acting so silly in front of Mr. Gordon. Something she would never do again! Not that she'd get the opportunity.

"You seem to be settling in just fine," Mr. Hancock said as he was leaving the office. "I really appreciate your efforts, Mrs. Clark."

"Thank you," she said a bit meekly.

"And you heard what Mr. Gordon said today." He shook a stern finger at her.

"What do you mean?" she asked nervously. Had he over-heard her conversation with the president?

"Everyone is expected to be at the Gordons' party tonight." He smiled. "That means you, too, Mrs. Clark."

"Oh . . . well, that's very kind, but I'm not sure I can make it."

"You're part of our team," he reminded her as he opened the glass door. "You heard what the boss said. Be there or be square." He laughed as he exited.

Caroline took time to straighten her desk, waiting until three fifteen to gather her things. Her hope was that most everyone would be gone by then. She simply wanted to slink out unnoticed. She even took the stairs instead of the elevator and was completely outside when she heard someone say her name.

"Mrs. Clark!" a male voice called.

She turned to see Mr. Gordon hurrying behind her, waving his hands as if he thought she'd just made off with the company's payroll. More likely, he simply wanted to fire her with little ado.

"Yes?" She stood her ground, waiting for the ax to fall, suspecting he was about to say they wouldn't need her to return on Wednesday.

"I'm glad I caught you," he said a bit breathlessly. "I saw you taking the stairs and—well, never mind. I just wanted to—"

"I'm so sorry," she burst out. "I was very disrespectful and unprofessional at lunchtime. I honestly had no idea who you were, Mr. Gordon. Not that it's an excuse. It certainly is not. I have no legitimate excuse. Except that I was a complete and utter fool. I do hope that you'll accept my most sincere apology." She fought to hold back her tears of frustration. She would not let him see her cry.

He blinked in surprise. "Well, yes, of course I accept your apology. But there's no need for that." He made a sheepish smile. "I actually enjoyed the whole charade. When you know me better, you'll understand that I'm a bit of a jokester myself. And, to be fair, I owe you an apology, too. I should've revealed my identity that day we met at the coffee shop. That was pretty thoughtless on my part. Not to mention bad manners."

"Oh . . . ?" She didn't want to show it, but that exact thought had gone through her head this afternoon. Why hadn't he given her his name the first time? Almost like he'd been playing cat and mouse.

"The reason I stopped you just now was to make sure you understood that you're invited to my parents' big bash tonight. I know you overheard me telling Evelyn that you were just temporary, and I'm sure it sounded all wrong. But I do hope you'll come tonight, Mrs. Clark. And, please, bring your husband, too."

She took in a quick breath. "My husband was killed in the war, Mr. Gordon."

His face grew somber. "I'm truly sorry for your loss. I didn't realize."

"Thank you." She tugged on the cuff of her glove. "He was a good man."

"I'm sure he was." His expression seemed full of concern now. "How long has it been since you lost him?"

"His plane was shot down fairly early on in the war. Almost four years now. It was in the South Pacific."

"I was in the Pacific theater, too," he said quietly.

"Really?" This caught her completely off guard. For some reason she'd imagined him running the chocolate factory throughout the war. But then again, she'd imagined the president to be much older, too—and not the same man she'd crossed paths with in the coffee shop. Apparently she was wrong about a number of things.

He glanced at his watch. "I hope we can continue this conversation later, but I promised to run some errands for my mother right now. You are coming to the big party tonight, aren't you?"

"Oh...I don't know..."

"Please, say you'll come, Mrs. Clark. Otherwise I'll feel guilty. As if my little prank has turned you against me for good."

Just then she remembered what everyone had been saying about team players. It was possible she would not be considered a team player if she snubbed their get-together tonight. And just when she was feeling a bit more hopeful about keeping her job, too. "Okay," she agreed. "I'd love to come."

"Good." He tipped his hat. "See you then."

Just as he turned to go in the other direction, Doris emerged from the building. "There you are," she called out as she joined Caroline. "Are you feeling better now? I was worried about you. It looked like you'd eaten a bad piece of fish."

Caroline laughed as they walked down the sidewalk together. "Yes, I'm feeling much better. Thank you for asking."

"And you're going to the big wingding tonight?" Doris paused under the striped awning of the chocolate shop to retrieve a set of car keys from her handbag.

"I guess so." She glanced over her shoulder. "Especially since the boss just insisted I should be there."

"Oh, that Mr. Gordon. He's such a good man. Always going out of his way to make people feel welcome and important. I just saw him talking to one of the janitors a bit ago, sincerely inquiring about his wife's ill health and telling him to pick up a box of chocolates—complimentary."

"That is nice."

Doris pointed across the street. "My car's over there. Need a ride?"

"No, I'm only a few blocks from here." She put her hand on Doris's arm. "Do you know how we're supposed to dress for tonight?"

"Oh, it's always very formal." Doris patted her hat. "I'm off to get my hair done right now."

"Formal?" Caroline felt her spirits sink.

"Oh, yes. You'll see sequins and satin and furs and the works. It's all very glamorous. Such fun, too!"

"And does everyone bring a date?"

"Not everyone." Doris grinned. "I'm not bringing anyone this year. I think it'll be more fun this way. Say, do you need a ride?"

"That would be wonderful."

They exchanged phone numbers, and Doris promised to pick her up at seven thirty sharp. Pausing to peer into her reflection of the chocolate shop window, Doris grimaced. "Good grief, I better get myself to the hairdresser's fast. I look like a wreck!"

As Doris hurried away, Caroline caught a glimpse of another image in the shop's gleaming window. Staring at her own reflection, she felt shocked. If she hadn't known better, she would've assumed that was her mother looking back! Maybe there was something to what her sister and a few of her coworkers had been suggesting to her after all.

Chapter 9

As Caroline went into her little apartment, she was overwhelmed with conflicted emotions. On one hand, she knew she should be thankful that her job was not in jeopardy. At least she didn't think it was. Not for six weeks anyway. On the other hand, she felt like she was in way over her head. The MG Chocolate Factory—at least the executive employees—was so sophisticated and worldly compared to what she'd been used to. And compared to the other secretaries, including Mrs. Gallagher, who was probably in her late fifties, Caroline was a dowdy, mousy, frumpy plain Jane.

Oh, she knew that appearances were deceiving. And she knew she was a good, steady, reliable worker. But she also knew that she'd stuck out like a sore thumb today. And now she was expected to come up with an appropriate outfit to wear to the formal New Year's Eve party tonight. She looked through her spartan closet, trying to determine if there was something in there she might be able to make over into some sort of an evening gown. But without a magic wand, it looked impossible. Perhaps the wise choice would be to simply stay home. Or was that the coward's way out?

"Hello? Caroline?" Marjorie called from the top of the stairs. "Joe said he saw you coming home—you down there?"

"I am."

"Well, come on up here. Lulu's still napping and I want to show you something."

Caroline barely reached the top of the stairs when Marjorie grabbed her by the hand. "Come on, Sis. Let's hurry before Lulu wakes up."

"Where are the boys?" Caroline whispered as they started up the stairs.

"Joe took Danny outside after his nap. I gave them a picnic snack to eat out there."

"Well, you are just the one I need to talk to," Caroline said quietly. "Turns out you were right about my fashion sense. Or lack of it. Seems that I need to improve my image."

"That is exactly what I have in mind." Marjorie pulled Caroline into her bedroom where the bed was piled with clothes.

"Are you packing to go somewhere?" Caroline picked up a pretty pink blouse.

"No. These are the clothes that are already too small for me." Marjorie patted her rounded midsection. "And I got to thinking it's a shame to have them just sitting in my closet. Meanwhile my sister is running around town looking like the war's still on."

Caroline sighed. "Point taken."

Marjorie held up a periwinkle peplum jacket and matching skirt. "I just got this a few months ago. On sale at Miss Beverly's Fine Fashions. I only wore it once. To a luncheon with Rich's mother."

"Very pretty."

Marjorie held the jacket up to Caroline. "It will look lovely on you."

"Oh, Marjorie, I can't take your new suit. You'll want it back after the—"

"It's just a loan," Marjorie explained. "You can use these things until you can afford to update your own wardrobe. And it will be good to get them out of my closet. It only makes me sad to see them there." She grabbed a handful and thrust them toward Caroline. "For all I know, they'll be out of style by the time I can fit into them again."

"This is so incredibly generous."

"Well, you used to give me your hand-me-downs," Marjorie reminded her. "I always acted like it wasn't fair that I had to wear secondhand clothes, but the truth was I loved having your things. I used to think you had real style back then. Back before...well, before the war and everything. You know..."

"I know." Caroline felt her eyes getting misty. "This is really sweet of you, Marjorie. I honestly don't know how to thank you."

"Well, just take good care of them." She chuckled. "I know you will. You were always much more careful with clothes than I was. Even that short stint I did for the modeling agency, I would get hecky-pecky for not handling garments properly."

Caroline laughed. "Yes, that was one reason I preferred to just give you my older clothes than to lend them to you. I never knew what kind of shape they'd come back in." She held up a cheery red dress with small white polka dots. "This is fun."

"I outgrew that waistline right after Thanksgiving," Marjorie admitted. "But it ought to fit you perfectly." She pulled out the full skirt. "And the hemline is much more fashionable than *that*." She pointed to Caroline's gray skirt.

"So I've gathered." Caroline told Marjorie about how stylish the other secretaries looked today. "Next to them I was a dowdy duck."

"It's possible they were dressed more colorfully than usual because it's New Year's Eve," Marjorie told her. "I mean I've seen some of them before and I'll admit they're rather chic, but they probably don't always dress up so much."

"Speaking of New Year's Eve..." Caroline told Marjorie about the party at the Gordon home. "Won't you and Rich want to go?"

Marjorie frowned. "Some day we'll go. At least I hope so. But not until Rich gets a big promotion and moves up to the executive offices."

"Oh...well, I didn't really want to go, but Mr. Gordon went to a special effort to make sure I knew I was invited." She felt her cheeks warming. "I mean because I'm a temporary employee, you know? He thought I might not feel like I belonged there."

"Mr. Gordon invited you personally?" Marjorie's eyes grew wide. *"Himself?"*

"Yes. I was on my way home. He ran out onto the sidewalk and stopped me."

"He *ran?*"

"Well, maybe he didn't actually run. I mean he sort of rushed out."

"Oh, Caroline, I'll bet he likes you."

"I'm sure he likes all his employees. He seems like a very nice man."

Marjorie grabbed Caroline's hand. "Do you *like* him?"

"Well, of course I like him. He's the president of the company."

"You know what I mean, Sis."

Caroline's cheeks grew even warmer.

"Look at you—you're blushing." Marjorie forced Caroline in front of her big dresser mirror. "You do like him, don't you? You can tell me."

Caroline's hand went up to her cheek. "Oh...I don't know...I suppose I sort of like him. I mean that sounds so silly...childish even."

"That's wonderful!"

Caroline laughed nervously. "Why is that wonderful? You know as well as I do that my chances with a man like Mr. Gordon would be minuscule...especially with someone like Evelyn Stuart around. I'm pretty sure that those two are a pair. I even heard some of the girls at work are wagering that he will propose to her by Valentine's Day."

Marjorie frowned. "Well, that doesn't give you a whole lot of time, now does it?"

"I don't think time is going to help." Caroline leaned forward to peer at her frumpy image in the mirror. "The bathroom mirror in the apartment is a bit cloudy," she confessed as she touched her hair. "I think my hair looked better in it down there."

Marjorie chuckled. "At least that's an easy fix." She reached for a hairbrush and immediately began unpinning Caroline's thick auburn hair. "You brush it out while I get something from the guest room closet."

By the time Caroline had brushed her hair out, letting it fall loose upon her shoulders, Marjorie returned with a long garment bag in hand. "I got this when I was working at the modeling agency, before the war began." Her voice was laced with excitement. "I nearly forgot about it. I haven't worn it since before Danny was born, and I'm afraid it might be a bit out of fashion by now. But perhaps we can do something about that." She slowly unzipped the bag and a full skirt of rich garnet-colored satin poured out.

"Oh, Marjorie." Caroline felt her eyes growing large. "That is lovely."

"Wait until you see the rest of it." She carefully extracted it from the bag, holding it out like a prize. The fitted bodice sparkled with garnet-colored sequins and looked like something that might've been worn in a movie. "It was a little snug on me after I had Danny, but I'm sure it'll fit you perfectly."

"It's beautiful." Caroline ran her hand down the shiny skirt. "Just beautiful."

"I was wearing it when I met Rich." Marjorie held the gown up to herself and sighed. "The modeling agency had sent some of us girls to work at an awards ceremony, something to do with the film industry, but not the Academy Awards. Anyway, we wore designer gowns, and afterward, we were allowed to purchase them with a really big discount." She laughed. "I used all my earnings just to buy this silly old gown."

"I can understand why." Caroline stared at the gorgeous garment. The style was classic, with a sweetheart neckline and fitted three-quarter-length sleeves. And the full skirt poured out in luscious billows of satin.

"Naturally, I had to come up with an excuse to wear it again." Still holding the gown to her, Marjorie waltzed around the bedroom.

"Naturally." Caroline smiled at her younger sister.

"Which is why some of us girls—from the agency— decided to go to a USO Christmas party. We wanted to show off. And, of course, we were dressed to the nines. And, as you know, that's where I met Rich." She laughed. "The rest is history."

"Well, this gown is absolutely gorgeous. And I can't imagine why you'd think it was out of fashion. I realize I'm not an expert, but I don't think a classic sort of dress like this could ever be out of style."

"Maybe...but it's not as flashy as some of the gowns I've been seeing in movies and magazines lately." She held it up to Caroline now, nodding with approval.

"Well, it has plenty of flash for someone like me." Caroline giggled. "Honestly, Marjorie, I feel like I'm about seventeen again, getting ready for my class prom."

"It's about time you had some fun." Marjorie removed it from the padded hanger. "Let's get you out of that old-lady suit and see how this looks."

"Do you really think it'll fit me?" Caroline hurried to unbutton her jacket.

"Well, you know we're nearly the same size, although I'm a little shorter than you, but I wore it with a sweet pair of matching high heels. Maybe you could wear it with a lower heel." Marjorie already had the back opened up.

"I don't own a pair of shoes that would look right with this dress, and you know my feet are bigger than yours."

"Looks like you'll have to go shoe shopping."

By seven thirty Caroline was elegantly dressed. Besides the garnet gown and a new pair of black patent leather pumps, she wore a pair of borrowed garnet earrings and a black fur stole. Marjorie had helped pin her hair into a looser, more feminine style and insisted she wear a touch of lipstick and rouge. "I feel just like Cinderella," she nervously told Marjorie as they waited in the front room for Doris to arrive.

"You look like a movie star." Joe looked at her with wide eyes. "I can't believe you're really my mom."

"Thanks, sweetheart. I actually feel a little silly," she confessed. "I'm not used to dressing up like this."

"Is that your friend?" Marjorie pointed to the light blue car pulling into the driveway.

"Looks like it." Caroline thanked Marjorie once more, then bent down to kiss Joe on the cheek, wiping off the lipstick smudge and smiling. "I know you'll be good for Aunt Marjorie. And you'll go to bed when she says to."

He nodded. "Have fun at your party, Mom."

"I'll try." As she hurried out to Doris's car, she had no idea what to expect and desperately hoped that she wasn't overdressed. She felt somewhat relieved to see that Doris had on a formal gown, too, a shimmering confection of pink and blue. But still, she felt uneasy.

"This all feels so strange to me," Caroline admitted as Doris took a winding road that went up a hill. "As if I'm someone else...not me."

"Wait until you see the Gordons' home," Doris said as she turned into a long driveway. "Then you'll really feel like you're someone else."

The Gordon home was stucco like Marjorie's, but it was enormous and all lit up with cars pulling in and guests piling out. A parking valet took Doris's keys, and the next thing Caroline knew they were walking through the big double doors, going into an enormous foyer that resembled something from a Hollywood movie set.

"Welcome," Mr. Gordon graciously greeted them both, politely introducing Caroline to his father as a young man collected their wraps. "Mr. Maxwell Gordon, the founder of MG Chocolates," he said proudly. Both men wore nearly identical black tuxedos and both looked very elegant—the young and the old. And now Caroline began to feel slightly more comfortable in her formal gown. She wasn't the least bit over-dressed.

"Pleased to meet you, Mrs. Clark," the senior Mr. Gordon told her. "And good to see you again, Miss Fowler. Welcome—welcome! Please, make yourselves at home."

"My mother had hoped to be out here to greet the guests, too," the younger Mr. Gordon explained to them, "but she twisted her ankle earlier."

"Oh, I'm sorry," Caroline said.

"But I know she'd like to meet a new employee," he said. "If you don't mind, I'll take you to her."

"I'd love to meet her." Caroline turned to Doris. "Are you coming, too?"

But Doris was already waving to a small group of people that Caroline didn't know. "I'll catch up with Mrs. Gordon later," Doris assured her as she hurried away.

Caroline tried to act natural as Mr. Gordon led her through a large room where a band was playing on one end and numerous guests were visiting on the other. But everything was so foreign, so unexpected, she felt as if she were part of a movie set.

"I'm so glad you made it," Mr. Gordon told her as they exited the busy room, going down a quiet hallway with artwork along both walls. He paused to look at her, and unless she was mistaken, he seemed to approve. A smile turned up the corners of his mouth and his dark eyes lit up. "You look very lovely tonight, Mrs. Clark."

She felt herself blushing again. "Thank you, Mr. Gordon. To be honest, I'm not used to such formal affairs. I'm a bit like a fish out of water."

"A most beautiful fish." He chuckled as he pulled open a door. "My mother is in the parlor, keeping her foot elevated for a bit. She hopes to get in at least one dance with my father before this year comes to an end." He nodded to where a pair of older women were seated comfortably near a large window that overlooked a pretty garden area. "Mother," he said as they approached. "I'd like you to meet our newest employee, Mrs. Clark. She's recently relocated here from Minnesota. She was just hired today." He smiled at Caroline. "This is my mother, Mrs. Gordon."

"Pleased to meet you." Caroline leaned down to grasp the older woman's hand. "You have a beautiful home, Mrs. Gordon."

"Please, just call me Gladdie," she said. "I never went in for all this formality."

"Then you must call me Caroline," she said, feeling a bit uneasy.

"And this is my sister, Beulah Peterson," Gladdie said pleasantly.

Caroline smiled at the older woman. "Pleased to meet you, too."

"Now, have a seat, Caroline." Gladdie patted a spot beside her. "Let's get acquainted."

Caroline glanced back at Mr. Gordon with uncertainty. What was she supposed to do?

"Go ahead and join them," he said. "And if you'll all excuse me, I better get back to help Dad greet the other guests."

"I thought Evelyn was helping with that," Gladdie said.

"She was, but she stepped out for a bit."

"Come on, Caroline," Gladdie urged her. "Sit down and keep us old ladies company. Tell us about Minnesota and what brings you out to our part of the country."

Caroline sat down next to Gladdie, smiling at the pair of friendly gray-haired women. "There's not much to tell about Minnesota." She tried to think of something interesting. "When I left there was quite a bit of snow on the ground."

"*Snow*," Beulah said with longing. "Remember back in Connecticut, that winter when we had five feet of snow?"

"Oh, I don't believe we ever had *five* feet of snow, Beulah." And for the next couple of minutes they argued back and forth over the Connecticut winters. But finally Gladdie turned back to Caroline. "I'm sorry, dear. You know how contrary sisters can be sometimes. Or perhaps you don't. Do you have a sister?"

So Caroline explained that she did indeed have a sister. "That was what drew me out to California...to be closer to her and her family."

"And your husband?" Gladdie asked. "My son did introduce you as *Mrs.* Clark, did he not?"

So Caroline quickly explained about losing Joe in the war. "It was early on...about four years ago...he was in the South Pacific."

Gladdie reached over to take Caroline's hand. "I'm so sorry for your loss, dear. So very sorry."

"Gladdie lost a boy to the war, too," Beulah said quietly. "Her older son—Max Jr."

"Oh, yes, I do remember my brother-in-law mentioning that now. I'm so sorry for your loss." Caroline looked into Gladdie's eyes. "It's hard, isn't it?"

She nodded. "Max Jr. was a good boy. He'd been running the company before he went into the service," Gladdie explained. "Alongside his father, Maxwell, of course. But Max Jr. had been Maxwell's right-hand man."

"The plan was for Max Jr. to take over the business entirely," Beulah filled in. "After the war. Such a tragedy when he was killed in France. So sad."

"A parent never expects to outlive a child." Gladdie shook her head. "Did you and your husband have any children, Caroline?"

"We have a son. Joseph Jr. Now he wants to go by Joe. He's almost ten, but quite grown-up for his age."

"You have a ten-year-old son?" Gladdie looked surprised. "You don't look old enough to have a boy that big."

"Young people nowadays," Beulah said, "they seem younger than we did at their age. Maybe it's the modern clothes they wear."

"Well, you're blessed to have a son, Caroline. Something no mother should take for granted. Especially when war can change everything in a heartbeat. I always thought I'd have both my two boys far into my old age. I imagined them with wives and children, filling this house with laughter and happiness." She sighed.

"I still remember Max and Terrence as little boys," Beulah said. "They were such opposites.

"That's for certain." Gladdie smiled. "Max Jr. was quiet and responsible, and Terrence was loud and rambunctious. And yet they were devoted to each other."

"Unless they were fighting," Beulah added with a sly grin.

"They rarely fought," Gladdie declared.

"And after Max Jr. was killed in France, Terrence offered to come home and work in the chocolate factory for his parents," Beulah told Caroline. "So generous of him. But he is a generous man. Always looking out for others. Like you." She pointed to Caroline. "Leave it to Terrence to see that you got to meet some of his family. Instead of just letting you wilt in some corner like a wallflower." She chuckled.

"Terrence has always been thoughtful like that," Gladdie said. "In many ways he's perfectly suited to manage a large company. Although it was never his dream to work in an office." Gladdie sighed. "You see, he was always my happy-go-lucky adventurer. Always longing to see the world and do exciting things. Even before the war, he trained as a pilot and went flying all over the place. He was working down in South America before the war broke out."

"The Army Air Corps was real glad to snatch him up, too," Beulah said. "Not many young men already knew how to fly an airplane like Terrence did."

"And now the poor boy is stuck running the chocolate factory." Gladdie pursed her lips. "I keep telling Maxwell that it won't last long. Terrence is going to start longing for adventures any time now. Next thing we know, he'll be shooting off to Argentina or Thailand or Timbuktu."

"No, no, I don't think so," Beulah countered. "I think the boy's settled down nicely since the war. He really cares about his employees. He's enjoying the challenges of making chocolate. You'll see, Gladdie."

"What do *you* think?" Gladdie suddenly asked Caroline.

"Goodness, I have no idea. To be honest, I barely know Mr. Gordon."

"*Terrence*," Gladdie told her.

"Yes, well, as I said, I barely know him."

"Then you should get to know him better," Beulah declared. "Terrence is a good boy. Always has been. Even if he has an adventurous spirit. Nothing wrong with that. Adds a little spice to life."

Caroline listened with interest as the two older women bantered back and forth. She contributed bits and pieces when it seemed appropriate, but mostly she just enjoyed hearing snippets about Terrence and more of the Gordon family history. The Gordons might be wealthy and influential, but from what she could see, they were just as normal as her own family. Perhaps even more so. And these two older ladies were truly a delight.

Chapter 10

You're still here." Mr. Gordon looked surprised to find Caroline right where he'd left her. "Have you been here the whole time?"

"Yes, but I've enjoyed it."

"But it's been more than an hour." His brow creased.

"You make it sound as if we've been torturing the poor girl," Gladdie said to him. "We've simply been getting better acquainted."

"That's right," Beulah added. "Caroline is an interesting young woman."

"And did you know she goes to our church?" his mother asked.

"As a matter of fact, yes." He grinned at Caroline, reaching for her hand. "How about if I rescue you by inviting you to the dance floor."

Gladdie clapped her hands. "Splendid idea, son."

"Yes," Beulah agreed. "By all means, go and dance with the girl. What are you waiting for anyway?"

"I've enjoyed chatting with both of you," Caroline called over her shoulder. "I hope your ankle is well enough to dance, Mrs. Gordon."

"*Gladdie*," she called back.

"I'm sorry for abandoning you with them for so long." Terrence was escorting her back toward the sound of the music. "Did you get anything to eat yet?"

"No, but I'm not particularly hungry."

"You would like to dance, though? Or did you simply agree in order to make a handy escape?"

"I'd love to dance." She felt uneasy. "But I must admit I haven't danced in years. I'm probably rather rusty."

"Then you're in good company."

Suddenly they were on the dance floor and, as if in a dream, he was taking her into his arms. But they'd barely started to dance when the song ended. "Shall we wait for the next number?" he asked with what seemed a hopeful expression.

"Yes, I'd love to. I felt like I was about to get the swing of it."

The next song was "String of Pearls," and, thanks to the familiar and steady beat, Caroline felt all the dance moves coming back to her, almost as if she'd stepped back in time. "I thought you said you were rusty," Terrence said when the music ended.

"That song made it easy."

Now the band was starting to play "Moonlight Serenade." "Want to try one more?" Terrence asked.

"I'd love to."

Since this song was slower, they were able to actually talk as they danced. "I do feel bad making you get stuck with the old ladies for so long," he apologized.

She smiled up at him. "The truth is I was probably more comfortable with them than I am with this large crowd." She glanced at the younger people dancing all around them. "I suppose I've gotten a little rusty at social gatherings, too."

"Well, if that's anything like your dancing skills, I wouldn't be too worried."

She laughed as he twirled her around. She couldn't remember the last time she'd had this much fun. But just as he pulled her back into his arms, she noticed something that spoiled it all. There, standing along the sidelines with a couple of attractive men, was Evelyn. Dressed in a low-cut gown of glittering pale blue, she held a glass of Champagne in one hand and a cigarette in the other. Her lips were smiling, but her eyes were not. And as she stared at Caroline and Terrence, her expression was so icy that Caroline felt an actual chill run down her spine.

"Want to go again?" Terrence asked hopefully as the song ended.

"I, uh, I don't know." She glanced back at Evelyn. "I don't want to monopolize all your time, Mr. Gordon. I realize you have other employees and—"

"This isn't the workplace." He laughed. "It's a party. And I can spend my time as I like."

"Yes." She nodded. "Of course you can."

"I'll bet you're hungry. I know I am. Let's go over and fill a plate while the buffet table isn't so busy."

She actually was hungry. Not only had she missed out on lunch, but she'd barely had anything for dinner as well. Even so, she felt so nervous that she wasn't sure she'd be able to eat now. Just the same, she let Terrence lead her along the buffet table, filling her plate with tempting appetizers.

"I don't know about you," he said as he handed her a glass of Champagne, "but I don't like standing to eat. Or eating amongst a crowd."

She nodded eagerly. "I'm the same."

"Come on." He tipped his head toward a side door and before long, they were walking along a patio that bordered a turquoise swimming pool.

"It's beautiful out here," she said as they strolled along.

"If it were warmer, I'd suggest we eat out here."

"It must be delightful to dine out here." She looked longingly at the pool. "So different from Minneapolis right now."

"I'll bet." He opened a door. "Right this way, Mrs. Clark."

She longed to tell him he could call her Caroline, but worried that might sound overly familiar. Besides that, she was already feeling uncomfortable about being this far from the other party guests—and alone with the boss. Not that she didn't trust him. For some reason she did. But she didn't want to give him—or anyone—the wrong impression. He led her into what appeared to be a billiards room. "How about this?"

"A pool table," she exclaimed. "What fun!"

"You play pool?"

"A little." She smiled as he pulled a couple of leather club chairs up to a small round table, pointing to one for her. As they both sat down, he lifted his glass. "Here's to you having a good first year in California, Mrs. Clark."

"Thank you." She clinked her glass into his, then took a tiny sip, giggling as the bubbles tickled her nose. "I haven't had Champagne in years."

"To be honest, I haven't either."

"Really?" Somehow she found this difficult to believe.

"You probably assume I live the big life all the time." He picked up an appetizer. "The truth is I've been living a fairly simple life . . . ever since the war ended." His expression darkened. "Sometimes it's hard to feel too celebratory."

"I understand." She nodded. "Your mother told me about losing your brother. I'm so sorry."

"I guess we've all had our losses."

"And we can be thankful that the war is over." She sighed. "It's hard to believe that just one year ago, it was still going strong."

He lifted his glass again. "Here's to 1946 being a good year for everyone."

As their glasses clinked together she smiled. "I also heard from your mother and aunt that you are a pilot. That must be exciting."

His face brightened. "I haven't been up in months, but I do love to fly."

"My son, Joe, dreams of becoming a pilot. He has a model plane collection."

"The opportunities for pilots should only be increasing as science and technology catch up."

As they ate, she asked him questions about planes and flying. She inquired about the places he'd visited, and listened with interest as he described exotic locales. "It all sounds so interesting," she said as they finished up. "You've led such an adventurous life." She tilted her head to one side. "It seems incongruous that you'd want to work in a factory."

He shrugged. "Well, you do what you have to."

"Yes, I'm well aware of that."

He looked intently at her. "I'm sure you are."

"But someone else could run the chocolate factory," she said quietly. "You're free to do pretty much as you please."

"Yes, I always thought so, too. The truth is I've led a fairly privileged life. And I suppose I've taken full advantage of it." He leaned back in the club chair, folding his arms across his front. "But when my brother died, well, things changed. I suddenly had this new sense of responsibility and family loyalty. I felt I needed to make up for something." His eyes lit up. "And the truth is I've been sort of enjoying it." He paused, his expression shifting. "I came home about a year ago—right after Max died. My parents were devastated. We all were. But my father was hit particularly hard. He lost all interest in MG Chocolates."

"That's understandable."

"So I felt like it was up to me to rescue the family business, and, just like I do everything else, I jumped right in. Fortunately, my father had secured government contracts to provide chocolate bars to the GIs during the war, so we were fiscally healthy. But everything in the company seemed worn and outdated. Even the employees were weary. I started upgrading machinery, hiring more employees, and basically just taking the company up to a whole new level. In a way, that felt like an adventure in itself." He smiled. "And as you heard earlier, we had our best year ever."

"That must be rewarding."

"It is." He pushed his chair back and gave her a sly look. "You say you play pool?"

She grinned. "Well, I'm sure I'm a little rusty."

"Rusty as in your dancing skills?" he teased as he racked up the balls.

She went over to pick out a pool cue, pausing to chalk the tip. "I haven't played in years," she said. "My father taught me when I was a girl. He had a barbershop with an old billiard table in back." She chuckled. "It helped to keep his clients coming back."

"Your father sounds like a smart man." He hung up the triangle. "Stars and stripes?"

"Sure."

"Care to break?"

"You go ahead." She watched as he sent the balls flying across the table. Two went in: one stripe, one solid. He went with stripes. She watched as he put two more balls in, then finally missed.

"Well, you did clean up the table a bit." She leaned over to take her first shot, sinking it easily.

"Nicely done."

And then, since he'd done such a good job of clearing the table, she put in two more shots.

"If this is you playing rusty, I'd better watch out."

She laughed as she watched him plan his next shot. He sunk one and missed one, leaving her with an easy shot. She put that in, as well as the next one.

"Excellent shooting, Mrs. Clark. I had no idea you'd be this much competition."

She only had one ball left. And when she missed, she wondered if she'd done it intentionally. It seemed rude to beat your host. He was just taking his next shot when the door burst open, causing him to pull up on his cue and miss.

"There you are!" Evelyn exclaimed as she bustled into the billiards room like a pale blue cyclone. "I've been looking all over for you, Terry. What on earth are you doing holed up down here of all places?" She shook her head. "And playing billiards by yourself?"

He pointed his cue to where Caroline was standing in the shadows on the opposite side of the table, obviously out of Evelyn's line of vision. "We were just having a little game of stars and stripes," he said lightly.

"Really?" Evelyn turned to see Caroline, staring in disbelief. "Oh? I had no idea. Well, good grief, I hope I'm not interrupting anything."

"I'm sure Mr. Gordon is relieved for the interruption," Caroline said in a teasing tone as she laid down her cue. "One more turn and I might've won."

"Wait a minute," Terrence said to her. "We're not done here yet."

"Oh, yes, you are." Evelyn took his cue and laid it on the table. "You have guests out there, Terry. Important people who want to talk to you. You can't hermit away like this—playing your little boy games."

Caroline exchanged a glance with Terrence. "Thank you for a lovely time," she said quietly. "And I do apologize," she said to Evelyn, "for keeping him from his guests."

Evelyn looked like she wanted to spit. Instead, she just smiled. "Well, Terry is always so thoughtful of new employees. Almost to a fault." She linked her arm in Terrence's. "Now come along, naughty boy. I promised your father I'd bring you back to the festivities."

He protested, but Caroline just waved at him, assuring him that she would find her way back just fine. "It'll give me a chance to look around a bit," she said as they were leaving. "I barely saw the art along that hallway."

"Yes," he called back, "feel free to look around—make yourself at home."

Caroline honestly did not know what to think as she walked back the way he'd brought her, alongside the pretty swimming pool, then down the art-filled hall. All the attention he'd given her was far more than she'd ever expected. And, really, it seemed a bit much, especially for a new employee—a temporary one at that. She suddenly remembered something Marjorie had said about women trailing after Mr. Gordon, that he could have his pick of any. Was that Marjorie's way of saying that he was a bit of a cad? Although he really didn't seem like a cad. He seemed genuine and caring and . . . well, just plain wonderful.

But perhaps there was more between him and Evelyn than

she realized. After all, there was gossip about them at the chocolate factory. And Caroline had seen them at church together. And Evelyn certainly appeared to be on intimate terms with his family, not to mention she was quite familiar and friendly with Terrence himself—or *Terry*, as she preferred to call him.

Instead of returning to the ballroom area, Caroline decided to stop by the parlor to check on Gladdie and Beulah. Suddenly their company—especially compared to Evelyn the Ice Queen—sounded delightful. But when she found her way back to the parlor, only Gladdie was there, quietly reading a magazine.

"Sorry to disturb you," Caroline apologized.

Gladdie looked up, removed her glasses, and smiled. "You're not a disturbance, dear girl. I simply sent Beulah to fetch us some dessert. Have you had any?"

"Not yet, but I'm still full from the lovely buffet. Thank you."

"Come sit with me," Gladdie insisted. "Tell me if you danced with Terrence and whether he stepped on your toes or not."

So Caroline told her about dancing and how they both did better than expected. She even went on to tell about the billiards game and how she very nearly beat him.

"But then he went on to win," Gladdie said with dismay.

"Not at all." Caroline explained about their interruption. "Of course, Miss Stuart insisted on taking him back to the other guests, which was understandable. And, really, I didn't mean to monopolize his time."

"Ha! I know my Terrence well enough to know he wouldn't let *anyone* monopolize his time unless he was enjoying himself, too."

"Oh..." Now Caroline didn't know what to say, and she felt a little guilty for telling his mother about this. It was almost as if she was tattling.

"Evelyn seems to have fixed her sights on Terrence," Gladdie said quietly. "And I suppose it's not terribly surprising... I mean after losing Max Jr., it's only natural that she should look to the other brother...I suppose."

Caroline considered this. "So Evelyn and Max Jr., uh, were romantically involved?"

"It's a bit complicated...but the short answer would be yes. You see, the Stuarts have been our dearest friends for years. We've known Evelyn since she was in diapers. And I suppose we parents had always imagined our families would be linked through the marriage of our children one day."

"I see." Caroline imagined a sort of monarchy.

"Evelyn always seemed more interested in Terrence than Max. But Terrence was always off doing something, flying planes, traveling to foreign countries. Max, on the other hand, had stuck around. And when Evelyn went to work at the chocolate factory, she and Max grew closer. Then Max went to war." She sighed.

Caroline patted her hand. "And war changes things." She repeated the exact words she'd heard Gladdie saying earlier.

"Yes, that's just right. It certainly does."

Just then Beulah returned with their desserts and Caroline excused herself, feigning interest in procuring a dessert, too, but in reality she simply wanted to go home. Suddenly and inexplicably, she felt exhausted. And, really, it had been an incredibly long day. So much had happened. So many feelings—highs and lows—that she felt emotionally drained.

Of course, as she walked along the perimeter of the dance floor area, she realized that her feet would probably sprout fresh wings if Terrence approached her for another dance. Was that even a possibility? She glanced over the crowd, hoping to see him coming her way. But when she spotted Terrence, he was dancing with Evelyn—and Caroline turned away, pretending not to have seen...not to have cared.

"Where have you been?" Doris asked her with arched brows. "I haven't seen you since we arrived."

"Oh...I had a nice visit with Mrs. Gordon and her sister..." Caroline glanced back to the dance floor, curious as to whether Terrence was enjoying himself, then chastising herself for caring.

"Don't they make a handsome couple," Doris said with a conspirator tone. "Isn't Miss Stuart's dress a knockout? Rumor is Mr. G might be planning a proposal for tonight. Wouldn't that be romantic? A New Year's Eve proposal? Oh, I think I would swoon if it was me."

"I guess that would be romantic." Caroline tried to sound oblivious. "But I heard that everyone is predicting he'll pop the question on Valentine's Day."

Doris laughed. "Your first day at MG and you've already heard about the pool?"

Caroline shrugged in an attempt at nonchalance. All she wanted was to go home now. She felt tired. Bone tired. But as she observed Doris, happily tapping her toes to the music, it was obvious her friend had no intention of leaving before midnight.

"I'm so worn out," she quietly told Doris. "I wonder if I should get a taxi and just call it a night."

"Don't bother with a taxi. The Gallaghers were just getting ready to leave," she told Caroline.

Caroline tried to recall why the name sounded familiar.

"*Georgia* Gallagher is Mr. Gordon's secretary, remember?"

Doris reminded her. "She and her husband were about to go home. Perhaps you can catch a ride."

"Thank you." Caroline forced a smile, then hurried out to the coat area, spotting Mrs. Gallagher being helped into her short fur jacket.

"Excuse me," Caroline said eagerly. "Doris just told me that you were heading home and that I could perhaps get a ride."

"Of course." Mrs. Gallagher pulled on her white gloves.

After Caroline gave her ticket to the young man, she quickly told the Gallaghers where she lived.

"You're right on our way," Mr. Gallagher assured her.

"You don't want to stay until midnight?" Mrs. Gallagher asked. "I thought all the young people stayed up late."

"It's been a very long day for me." Caroline tossed Marjorie's stole over her shoulders. "And I'd really like to be with my son...to wish him a happy New Year."

"Well, of course," Mrs. Gallagher said as they walked outside. "I don't blame you a bit."

As Mr. Gallagher drove them home, Mrs. Gallagher raved about her boss. "I wasn't sure that I'd like working for the younger Mr. Gordon," she said, "but I must say he's been a pure delight. MG Chocolates is very fortunate to have such a kind and caring man at its helm. I'd venture to say that everyone there loves him—and he loves them back. Such a good man."

Mr. Gallagher changed the subject by asking Caroline about herself. She explained about how her husband was a casualty of war, the age of her son, and why she'd moved out here to live with her sister and her family...finally sharing about her hopes to start a new life and anticipations for a good year ahead. But the truth was she mostly felt dismayed.

Chapter 11

On New Year's Day, Caroline was determined to begin the year with positive thoughts and hopeful feelings. She
started the morning by fixing a late breakfast for herself and
Joe. And she was just about to ask him about spending the
rest of the day with her when he announced that he wanted to
go visit his new friend Jimmy Rolland today.

"But New Year's Day is sort of a holiday," she said weakly.

"Aunt Marjorie said they're not doing anything special,
just sleeping in and stuff," he told her. "And she let me call
Jimmy yesterday, and Jimmy invited me to come over to play
ball with him and his buddies."

"Ball?"

"Yeah. Jimmy's dad and uncle and some of his cousins and
neighborhood kids, they all get together to play football on
New Year's Day. It's a tradition."

"Oh..." She frowned at Joe. "Football? Isn't that kind of
dangerous?"

"It's just touch football," he told her.

"You really want to go?"

He eagerly nodded.

"All right. But you write down Jimmy's address and phone number for me," she told him. "Since I haven't met his parents yet."

After Joe went off to Jimmy's house and she'd returned Marjorie's Cinderella outfit, assuring her that she'd enjoyed the New Year's Eve party, Caroline went back down to her apartment and did some routine cleaning. But after a bit, she found herself repeating chores that didn't need doing, and she realized that the apartment was clean enough. Feeling antsy and unsettled, she paced back and forth, pausing now and then to glance at the sunny, clear day outside. She suddenly felt like a caged squirrel. She had to get out of there!

She went to her closet, where she'd already hung all the gorgeous clothes that Marjorie had so generously shared. She flipped through the garments until she came to the red and white polka-dot dress. She pulled it out, admiring the nice full skirt and the crisp white belt that would go around the fitted waist. This would never be a work dress. Not for her anyway. But it seemed a good "Saturday" dress. At least what she used to call a Saturday dress. And although today wasn't Saturday, it felt sort of like it.

And so she put on the dress along with the lower-heeled black pumps she'd gotten yesterday. And then she let her hair down so it curled loosely around her shoulders. But then she pinned the front part up, similar to how Marjorie had fixed it yesterday.

"All dressed up and no place to go." She smiled at her surprisingly cheerful image in the somewhat dim bathroom mirror. Why not take a walk? She doubted that anything in town would be open on New Year's Day, but she could window-shop and get some fresh air.

She felt her spirits lighten as she strolled to town. Something about wearing a pretty dress on a sunny day was uplifting. She walked past Dee Dee's Coffee Shop, which was closed. Past Speckled Hen Groceries and Dorn Brothers Shoes, where she'd gotten her black pumps yesterday. All were closed. But she didn't really care. She walked past MG Chocolates, too, and past the chocolate shop, which she'd yet to visit, and they were closed, too. She was about to turn around and go home when she noticed that the Black and White Café was open across the street. She wasn't hungry for lunch yet, but when she saw the SODAS sign, she decided to investigate.

The bell on the door jingled as she went inside. Cheerful black and white checkerboard floors and aqua-blue booths greeted her, as well as a plump middle-aged woman in a black and white uniform. "Take any seat you like," she called out. "As you can see, we're not exactly packed yet."

"But at least you're open." As Caroline slid into a booth by the window, she realized she was the only customer.

"I was just wondering if that was a mistake." The woman glumly set down a menu. "But last year I got a lot of high school kids in here on New Year's Day." She shrugged. "You never know."

"I'm afraid I'm not terribly hungry," Caroline admitted. "But I would like a soda." She chuckled. "I haven't had one in years."

"What flavor?"

"Do you have strawberry?"

"You got it, honey."

As Caroline listened to the sound of the radio and whirring soda machine, she couldn't help but compare what she was doing right now to what she would be doing if she were still living in Minneapolis. Probably nothing. Perhaps knitting or reading. Or maybe getting ready to go have lunch at her parents'. As much as she missed them, she didn't regret her choice to come out here. Even sitting here by herself, waiting for her strawberry soda, seemed preferable to her previous life.

She sighed happily as she gazed out the window. Certainly, her life wasn't perfect and she still had plenty to figure out, but at this moment, she felt content...and very nearly happy. She smiled as she looked out the window, gazing out onto empty sidewalks. Across the way was MG Chocolate Factory. Interesting how it dominated the street...perhaps even the town. And for now, she was employed there. At least for six weeks. And maybe even after that if the company continued to expand the way everyone was predicting.

"Here you go, honey."

Caroline's eyes grew wide when she saw the gigantic strawberry soda mixed with ice cream and topped with a generous dollop of whipped cream in front of her. "Oh, my!"

"You looked like you could use the jumbo size." The waitress grinned. "Happy New Year."

Caroline thanked her and picked up her spoon. She was about to dip into it when she saw a figure exiting the chocolate factory. She leaned closer to the window, peering curiously at the man emerging onto the street. When she realized who it was, her heart seemed to skip a beat. Dressed in a gray business suit and matching hat, it appeared to be Terrence. *Rather, Mr. Gordon*, she reminded herself. Her boss.

Not wanting to be caught staring, she quickly turned away, focusing her attention on the decadent-looking soda in front of her. It was so big it was almost embarrassing. But when she tasted a bite, she realized she didn't care. It was delicious. Just as she was dipping her spoon in for a second bite, she heard the bell jingling, and when she looked up, she saw him.

"Hello," he said warmly, removing his hat as he entered. "I thought that was you."

"Oh, hello," she said, trying to appear calm and collected.

"That looks interesting," he said as he approached her table.

"It's actually quite good," she confessed. "But I had no idea it would be this big."

He tipped his head to the other side of her booth. "Is that seat taken?"

"No." She tried to keep her voice calm. "Please, feel free."

He slid into the seat, but as he did, his smile faded. "You seemed to have disappeared last night."

"Oh . . . yes . . ." She felt surprised he'd noticed. "I was tired. I caught a ride home with Mrs. Gallagher and her husband."

"Georgia took you home?"

She just nodded.

"You didn't even say goodbye."

"I'm sorry. I did speak to your mother. I believe I told her goodbye." But even as she said this she was unsure.

"Afternoon, Mr. Gordon." The waitress smiled brightly at him. "It's good to see you today."

"You, too, Nadine. You're looking well. I assume the holidays were good to you."

"Thank you." She patted her dark hair with a flirty smile. "No complaints. Now what can I get for you?"

He pointed to Caroline's soda. "I'll have what she's having."

"Coming right up."

He looked back at Caroline. "We never finished the billiards game."

She made a sly smile. "Maybe you should be relieved."

He nodded. "Yes, you weren't doing too badly."

"Well, I did feel bad for monopolizing your time," she said quietly. "When there were so many guests."

"I like to think that my time is my own when I'm not at work."

In her mind's eye she saw him dancing with Evelyn. "Yes, that seems fair."

They both grew quiet and Caroline couldn't think of anything to say. And then without really thinking, she spoke. "I heard that there might've been a big announcement last night. Hopefully I didn't miss anything important."

"An announcement?" He frowned.

"Well, it was just something someone said...probably nothing...just idle gossip." She focused her attention on the frothy pink drink in front of her, wishing she'd kept her mouth closed.

"Here you go, Mr. Gordon." The waitress set another strawberry soda down. "Happy New Year."

"You, too, Nadine." He held it up to her. "Here's to a really good year for the Black and White."

"Thank you, sir." She smoothed her hands down the skirt of her uniform, then walked away.

He sampled his soda, then smiled. "Hey, this really is good."

"Told you." She smiled, then began telling him about the first time she had a soda like this back in Minnesota. She knew exactly what she was doing, hoping to distract him from her nosy question. "And I haven't had a soda in years," she admitted. "I guess maybe I missed it." She smiled at him. "I'll bet there were a lot of things you missed during the war. What do you suppose you missed the most?"

Her tactic seemed to have worked, because he was suddenly telling her about all the various deprivations and the foods and things that servicemen used to daydream about. "But, of course, it was probably the people we missed most of all. Our family and friends back at home."

"Yes." She nodded. "I can understand that firsthand now. Well, certainly not like you experienced. But I've never lived far away from my parents before. And even though it's not even been a week, I miss them dearly."

They chatted congenially as they sipped their sodas, but eventually the tall glasses were empty, or nearly, and Caroline could tell this impromptu meeting was about to end. And judging by Terrence's suit, she suspected he was off to something of more importance than sharing a soda with a new employee.

"Before I go," he said as she pushed the empty glass aside, "I'm still curious about what you said earlier...you mentioned a rumor about a big announcement. Care to elaborate a bit?"

She felt her cheeks growing warm again. Why had she mentioned it? "Oh, it wasn't really anything."

"And here I thought you were my friend and that I could trust you." He gave her a slightly wounded look that reminded her of her son when he didn't get his way. It disarmed her when he'd called her his friend. And yet...

"If rumors are floating around, it only seems fair I should know about them," he persisted.

Naturally she felt even more torn. "Well, if you really must know, it was a rumor about you and Evelyn—I mean Miss Stuart."

His dark brows arched with interest. *"And... ?"*

"And the rumor was that perhaps you were going to announce your engagement to Miss Stuart last night. You know, for New Year's Eve." She made a little shrug.

"I see..." He was reaching for the check.

"Well, you know how people talk," she said apologetically. "It's fun for them to speculate about such things. I didn't really take it seriously."

"Was that why you left?" He looked intently into her eyes.

"No, of course not," she answered quickly. "The truth is I was very tired." As she reached for her handbag, extracting some change for her soda, she replayed all that had gone on in her world the past several days. "I really hadn't intended to go out last night. Despite it being New Year's Eve. And when the Gallaghers offered me a ride home, I gladly accepted." She started to lay her money on the table, but he stopped her.

"Let me." He laid three dollars on the check and picked up his hat. That was far more than the total even with a generous tip, but as he stood she could tell he intended to leave all of it.

"Well, thank you," she said as she stood. "I didn't expect—"

"Happy New Year, Mrs. Clark." His eyes twinkled as he put on his hat. "Have a good day."

"You, too," she said, pretending to be fussing with her handbag and gloves, but really just allowing him time to leave without her. For some reason, she felt like she needed that much space. Room to catch her breath and figure out what had just happened. He had never answered one way or the other about the big announcement, but for some reason she took that as a negative. If he were a newly engaged man, he surely would say something. And he surely wouldn't buy another girl a soda!

Chapter 12

Caroline felt on top of the world as she walked Joe
to his first day at his new school. Joe seemed happy, too. His
day spent playing football with Jimmy and his family and
neighbors had made him feel even more connected to the
neighborhood. She knew he was going to be fine. And after
she met the principal and Joe's new teacher, she controlled
herself and refrained from kissing Joe goodbye or saying anything to embarrass him.

"Have a great day." She waved as she watched him following Mrs. Trotter into his new classroom. "I'll see you after
work." He just grinned and waved back.

It was starting to cloud up as she walked to the MG Chocolate Factory. The radio weather forecast had predicted rain,
so she'd brought an umbrella, but she found it hard to believe
that this land of sunshine ever experienced real rain. She'd
dressed in one of the borrowed suits this morning, picking
a more conservative one since she was still concerned about

maintaining a professional image. That was something she'd learned in secretarial school, and despite the more casual styles the California women were sporting, she was still uneasy.

She glanced down at the brown-and-white-checked suit with satisfaction. It was the sort of outfit that would fit into most office situations, but pairing it with a rose-colored silk blouse made it seem a bit more fun. And although her hair was pinned up, it was in a looser, more casual style—something Marjorie had helped her with.

As Caroline entered the building, she greeted Miss Warner at the reception desk along with several other coworkers who were milling about. She was about ten minutes early, but that was typical of her work ethic. As she rode up the elevator with Mrs. Gallagher and two salesmen, they all chatted pleasantly. As they got out, going their separate ways, she felt amazed at how she already fit in here, like she was truly part of the MG team. At least for six weeks...possibly longer if all went well.

She went directly to her desk, picking up from where she'd left off on her first day. As the morning progressed, she took dictation on a number of letters, transcribed some other letters, sorted the mail, and answered the phone. All very routine, of course, but she did it all with careful professionalism. Her goal was to do this job so well that by the time Miss Bentley returned, she would be considered too valuable to part with. Even if it meant working on the assembly line or in the mail room.

At lunch she took her brown bag to the break room and, feeling a bit like the new kid at school, sighed with relief to see that Doris had saved her a place at a table. "You never took your coffee break?" Doris asked as Caroline sat down.

"I was so busy at work I forgot all about it."

Doris shook a friendly finger at her. "Don't make the rest of us look bad."

Caroline smiled as she opened her bag. "I'll be sure to take my breaks. I promise."

They visited companionably for a bit, then Caroline got up for a cup of coffee. As she was pouring in some cream, Terrence came into the room. Naturally, this brought a pleasant albeit unsettling sensation. But Caroline tried to appear perfectly at ease as she got a spoon to stir in the cream.

"Good afternoon," he said in a brisk business tone as he poured himself a cup of coffee.

"Good afternoon, Mr. Gordon," she answered politely.

"Are you settling in okay?" He glanced at her as he spooned some sugar into his cup. "Finding everything you need?"

"Yes. I'm feeling right at home." She smiled at him as she put her spoon in the sink.

"Good to hear." He smiled warmly back.

And before she could think of anything else to say, the door opened and Evelyn burst into the room, looking all around with a slightly frantic expression.

"There you are, Terry." Evelyn came directly to him. Dressed in an impeccable cream-colored suit, she paused to give Caroline a questioning glance, then turned back to Terrence. "I've been looking all over creation for you."

"Well, here I am. What can I do for you?"

Evelyn poured her own coffee, and Caroline could smell her perfume wafting over. And although Caroline was headed back to her table, she couldn't help but overhear Evelyn. "I need you to come to my office *immediately*," she said a bit sharply. "Something's come up regarding New York, and it's urgent. As in *right now* sort of urgent."

Caroline watched as Terrence, casually carrying his coffee, obediently followed Evelyn out of the break room. And it wasn't that Caroline didn't think Evelyn's problem was important; it was simply that Evelyn seemed to enjoy the drama a little too much. Or perhaps it was simply her way of keeping Terrence under her thumb. Although Caroline didn't perceive him as the kind of man who was easily dominated...by anyone. So if he was coming and going at Evelyn's beck and call, perhaps it was simply because he wanted to.

Caroline sat back down with Doris. "So I assume there were no proposal announcements on New Year's Eve," she said quietly.

Doris just shook her head. "Maybe Valentine's Day."

Somehow Caroline didn't think so. Or perhaps she was simply being overly optimistic. Or just delusional.

For the rest of the day, Caroline focused all her energy and attention on doing the best job possible, and when it was quitting time, Mr. Hancock commented on her work ethic. "So far I'm very impressed with your skills and how hard you work," he said. "Thank you."

"Thank you," she told him. It was actually very refreshing to have a boss who noticed such things, but she knew better than to make too much of the compliment. "I realize the company is in a busy time right now. I want to do all I can to keep the production department running smoothly."

"I appreciate it."

"And I was meaning to ask you," she said as he put on his hat, "would you like me to get you coffee in the morning? I used to do that for my other boss. I wouldn't mind doing that for you."

He gave her a grateful smile as he picked up his briefcase. "That would be very nice. Black with one spoonful of sugar."

"Have a good evening," she said as he reached for the door.

"Thanks. And, oh yes, I almost forgot, we're having an executive meeting Friday morning at ten. I'll need you in attendance to take notes."

"I'll put it on the schedule," she assured him.

On Friday morning, Caroline decided to wear the periwinkle suit with the peplum jacket. It was probably the most stylish suit in the clothes that Marjorie had insisted on loaning her, and as Caroline walked to work, she hoped it wasn't too much. She knew she'd be participating in the executive meeting, and she certainly didn't want to draw attention to herself. But then she remembered how chic Evelyn and her secretary were. And Doris was fairly fashionable, too.

"Oh, my," Miss Warner gushed as Caroline came into the foyer. "You look like a million bucks today."

Caroline made an embarrassed smile. "Thank you," she said quietly. "My sister insisted that I update my midwestern wardrobe." She lowered her voice even more. "This is actually hers." Miss Warner gave an approving nod as she reached for the ringing telephone. And as Caroline headed for the elevator, she held her head a bit higher. She was just pressing the up button when Terrence joined her.

"Good morning, Mrs. Clark." He smiled warmly at her.

"Good morning, Mr. Gordon." She felt a wave of relief that she hadn't called him Terrence, the way she was accustomed to thinking of him in her mind. That would be mortifying. Although there were a few others in the lobby, no one seemed interested in taking the elevator just yet, so it was only the two of them.

"I was surprised to see that it rained yesterday," she said as the doors closed. "It's been so sunny here that I was under the impression it never rained."

He chuckled as he pushed the button for the fourth floor. "Just wait. Sometimes we get such deluges that people start building boats."

"Next you'll be telling me that it snows, too," she teased back.

"So are you still settling in okay? Does your son like his new school?"

"He's happy as a clam. In fact, I was just marveling at it all this morning. Joe didn't even want me to walk to school with him. He was meeting his new friend halfway there, and they were walking together." She went on to tell about how Joe was getting interested in sports now. "He told me he's saving up to buy a baseball mitt." She shook her head. "But he doesn't even know how to play baseball."

"Getting the mitt is like a right of passage," he explained. "A boy doesn't have to know how to play baseball before he gets a mitt. But when he has his own mitt, he suddenly feels ready to take on the game. Sounds like he's doing it just right." He smiled as the doors opened. "Sounds like you're doing it just right, too."

Evelyn and Miss Thornton appeared to be waiting for the elevator. Both were wearing pink, although Evelyn's was a powdery pink and Miss Thornton's was magenta, but they looked good together. Almost as if they'd coordinated it. "Good morning, Terry," Evelyn said sweetly as Terrence moved aside to let Caroline out ahead of him.

"Good morning," Caroline politely told the two women as she passed by them, although neither of them had bothered to address her. However, they did return her greeting in a perfunctory way.

"Have a good day, Mrs. Clark," Terrence called out to her.

"Thank you." Caroline smiled brightly at him. "You, too."

"Good grief, Terry," Evelyn exclaimed as Caroline turned toward the production department. "Have you lost all your manners? I said good morning and you completely ignored me."

Caroline smiled to herself as she went into her office, taking her time to put her purse and gloves in the closet. Perhaps Terrence wasn't quite as interested in Evelyn as Evelyn appeared to be in him. As she sat down at her desk, she reminded herself that she was here to work—not to daydream about the big boss. Just the same, she couldn't help but think Terrence was being more than just professionally courteous to her. And when she allowed herself to replay the moments they'd had together, they did seem to add up to more than just a business friendship. Still, she wasn't sure. And this was not the time to speculate. Even so, she was glad she'd worn the periwinkle suit today. Unless she was mistaken, Terrence had liked it.

At just a minute before nine, when her workday officially began, she went to get Mr. Hancock his coffee. She was just adding one spoonful of sugar when Evelyn's assistant came in. "Oh, good," she said, "I was hoping to see you."

Caroline smiled at her. "Yes?"

"Miss Stuart told me to ask if you've read the employee manual yet." Miss Thornton poured coffee into a pink cup, adding two spoonfuls of sugar and stirring it vigorously.

"I noticed a copy of it in Miss Bentley's desk, but I haven't had a chance to read it yet," Caroline admitted.

"Well, Miss Stuart recommends that you do so as soon as possible." Miss Thornton dropped the spoon in the sink. "Particularly page nineteen. She thinks you should pay special attention to page nineteen." Miss Thornton had a somewhat smug-looking smile as she picked up the cup and headed for the door.

"Thank you," Caroline said with uncertainty as she rinsed both spoons, setting them in the drainer. She carried Mr. Hancock's coffee back to their department, setting it on the coaster on his desk just as he was coming in. They exchanged greetings, and he reminded her of the meeting and thanked her for the coffee.

Caroline attended to a couple of tasks, then opened the drawer where she'd seen what looked like a crisp copy of a never-opened pamphlet, *Maxwell Gordon Chocolate Factory, Employee Manual*. She opened it to see that the thin booklet was printed in 1933. Not exactly recently. She flipped through the pages, skimming what seemed like ordinary and reasonable expectations, until she came to page nineteen, which she read carefully. This section was titled "Relationships in the Workplace." And most of it was about things like manners and courtesy and settling grievances between coworkers. But it was the last paragraph about romantic relationships in the workplace that stopped her. According to this manual, they were expressly forbidden and grounds for immediate termination.

She slid the manual back into the drawer and sighed. Evelyn was obviously trying to send her a message. But why? Did she suspect that Caroline was pursuing Terrence? *Was* Caroline pursuing him? *No*, she told herself as she closed the drawer. Oh, certainly, she felt an attraction. And to her own surprise, she'd sensed herself opening to the possibilities. Not in a big way—more like a door that was barely cracked, letting just a slit of light inside.

But in reality, she probably felt more comfortable simply daydreaming about the whole thing. And, really, it seemed harmless, since a man like Terrence Gordon, on so many levels, seemed completely unattainable—and therefore safe.

Besides that, she simply liked him...as a friend. Yet if Evelyn felt the need to warn her like this, Caroline realized she should be more cautious. The last thing she needed was to lose a good job simply because she'd given someone the impression that she was flirting with the boss. That would be a disaster. Besides, she sternly reminded herself, Terrence Gordon was nice to everyone. Just because he had been extra kind to his newest employee didn't mean anything. It was simply his way.

When it was time for the executive meeting, Caroline was prepared with her steno pad and spare pencils. She'd also spent a couple minutes in the ladies' room, putting her hair into a tighter, more professional-looking, bun. Sure, Marjorie would say it made her look like an old lady, but Caroline didn't care. She needed to do whatever was necessary to avoid the appearance of seeking out a romance in the workplace. Never mind that she'd heard all sorts of snippets of conversations from other female employees—ones who appeared to be on the lookout for a husband—or even Evelyn, who seemed intent on keeping *Mr. Gordon* (as Caroline had now decided to think of him) to herself.

The executive meeting room was fairly typical. A long dark table with a number of comfortable-looking leather chairs around it, and then some less-comfortable-looking chairs against the walls. But covering the back wall, behind what she assumed was the head of the table, was a cheerful display of heart-shaped Valentine candy boxes, lending an air of fun to the otherwise serious room. As Mr. Hancock took a seat, she noticed several boxes of opened chocolates on the table, giving the place almost a party atmosphere. Caroline saw that Doris had taken one of the wall chairs, slightly behind her boss, so Caroline did the same.

Before long, all the VPs, Mr. Gordon, as well as the secre-

taries were seated and the meeting was called to order. Like the
other secretaries, Caroline kept her focus on her steno pad and
note taking as the meeting progressed. It seemed the biggest
discussion topic of the day was a new packaging design that
the marketing department had come up with for a candy box.

"This is not just an ordinary Valentine's candy box," Evelyn was explaining. "It's a statement." She held the model
up for all to see. It was a large heart-shaped box covered in
padded pink satin that resembled upholstery with clothcov-
ered buttons. It had a ruffled edge of satin and lace trim and a
dark pink velvet bow. "You give this to your girl and you are
saying something. *It's a statement.* It's not just a box of chocolates. It's so much more. *It's a statement.* A girl shows this off
to her friends, she is making *a statement.* This box is—"

"Okay, okay," Mr. Price said with a bit of irritation. "We
get that. The box is a statement. My question is, will it hold
up during shipment? You know we don't have refrigeration
on our trucks. And that fabric looks delicate. Like a disaster
just waiting to happen. For instance, down south, the weather
occasionally gets warm in February. What if the chocolate
melts a little? What if it ruins that fancy fabric? Then where
would we be?"

"The liner in the box will prevent that," she said impa-
tiently. "Just like with our other packages."

"But it's so late in the season to be introducing a new package. Especially a complicated one like that." Mr. Hancock's
tone sounded worried. "Why not save it for next year, when
we can take the proper time to do it right?"

"Because we have to beat out the competition," she told
him. "It's time to raise the bar. If MG wants to continue being
a big player in the confectionery world, we have to stay ahead
of the pack."

"I agree," Mr. Gordon said. "But you have to admit you're throwing this at us a bit late in the game."

"That's right," Mr. Hancock agreed. "We're not magicians, Miss Stuart. And to be honest, it feels like you're asking me to pull a rabbit out of my hat. We already have a challenging season ahead. Our production goals are larger than ever for January. My crew is functioning at full throttle already."

"I realize it will take a bit more time on the onset," she told him. "And I'm certainly not asking you to package *all* the Valentine's chocolates like this. But this box will be our star—our front-liner. I even wanted to run some sort of contest in New York next week. And perhaps a promotion—a store owner receives it complimentary if the order is sufficient."

"I like that!" Mr. Russell, the VP of Sales, nodded.

"Can't you just see some of these beauties in our display at the New York show?" she said to him. "I want to knock the socks off of the vendors this year. Can you imagine the orders you'd get with this new packaging?"

Mr. Russell slapped the table. "It's not like anything out there, Evelyn. You're right; it is a statement piece. I think we could double our sales with the promotion you're describing."

"Which is why we need to pull out all the stops and do this," she told everyone persuasively. "There's still time, we just have to get on it *immediately*."

"Is that possible?" Mr. Gordon asked Mr. Hancock. "Can you manufacture those boxes in time to get them into the stores at least two weeks before Valentine's Day?"

"I suppose anything is possible," Mr. Hancock said with reservation. "But it'll be a lot of work. I might have to hire more employees."

"Then do it," Evelyn exclaimed. Suddenly all the VPs were

talking at once. Production and Distribution were stating reasons of opposition while Marketing and Sales were off and running. Caroline could barely manage to get down all their comments.

"Okay," Mr. Gordon spoke loudly, getting everyone's attention. "Here's what I think we should do. As you know, the New York trade show is next week. Our full sales force will be there. We'll take prototypes of this new packaging and, if Evelyn and Glen are correct, if we really do double our orders, I will telephone you from New York." He pointed to Mr. Hancock. "And you will immediately go into production of the new packaging. Understood?"

"Okay, if that's what you want." Mr. Hancock still sounded doubtful. "But I want to go on record as saying I recommended we waited until next year."

"And I want to go on record saying that I'm concerned about the sturdiness of a package that's covered in a delicate fabric like that," Mr. Price added. "I won't take responsibility for chocolate that gets soft in warm temperatures and makes a mess of that satin. I remember when my wife spilled milk on a satin dress. Never did come out."

"Dear, dear Warren," Evelyn said in a teasing tone. "Such a worrier. Like a dog with a bone."

"You'd worry, too, if it was your responsibility to get something as delicate as chocolate to its final destination—and in perfect condition," he said back to her.

"And yet you do such an outstanding job." Her voice was sweet as syrup. "Year after year. You always deliver, Warren."

He chuckled. "Yep. Delivering, that's what I do."

Caroline wasn't sure how detailed Mr. Hancock wanted her notes to be, but just to be safe, she'd tried to get it all down. It had been a relief to have something to focus on besides Mr.

Gordon at the head of the table. Although she'd tried to keep her eyes on her steno pad, she couldn't help but notice how handsome he looked in his dark brown suit. And she admired the way he managed his VPs, somehow listening to all of them and making the decision he felt was best for the company.

The meeting ended, and as Caroline was finishing up her notes, she realized the other secretaries were already moving toward the door. She stood, too, making her way around the room, trying not to eavesdrop as the VPs and Mr. Gordon remained behind, chatting about the New York show.

"Okay, Terry, looks like you owe me a steak dinner in New York," Evelyn said in a flirtatious tone.

"That was your bet, not mine," he said good-naturedly. "Besides, you haven't won yet."

"Oh, I will win," she told him as Caroline reached the door. "You'll see. Don't I always win? And I won't settle for merely a New Yorker steak. I want a good bottle of Champagne, too." Her laughter seemed to follow Caroline out the door. There, Doris was waiting for her.

"Well, that was interesting," Doris said as they walked together. "I thought for sure that Mr. Gordon would agree with Mr. Hancock and put the kibosh on that crazy packaging plan." She shook her head. "Miss Stuart might be full of ideas, but she doesn't always understand the complications of carrying them out."

"It was a beautiful package," Caroline admitted.

"A *statement*," Doris said in a teasing tone.

"Let's just hope it's a good statement." Caroline chuckled as she went into the production department. And, although she wasn't particularly fond of Evelyn, she had to admit that her satin box idea was clever. The package was definitely attractive. It was the sort of box a girl would keep long after the chocolates were gone. Perhaps she'd use it as a jewelry box or a place to contain love letters. It really was a beautiful Valentine keepsake. And, for the sake of the company, Caroline hoped that it would be a success in New York. As she started sorting the morning mail, she tried not to imagine Mr. Gordon and Evelyn sharing a steak dinner and Champagne in a glamorous Manhattan restaurant. But, like a Technicolor film, it was all she could see playing through her mind.

Chapter 13

On Monday Caroline was determined not to let images of Evelyn and Mr. Gordon infiltrate her thoughts. However, as the day passed, unwanted scenes of the two of them would flash through her mind. In the morning she saw them flying together across the country on a luxurious airplane. In the afternoon, she saw them riding in the back of a taxi together. And as she walked home from work, she saw them in the lobby of a fancy New York hotel. Oh, she knew that Terrence was an honorable employer and would never take advantage of a situation like that. And she was fully aware that the two of them were not there alone. Plenty of other MG employees had gone as well. The VP of Sales and his sales team had left on the same flight. But somehow it was only Mr. Gordon and the glamorous Evelyn that starred in this troublesome movie that kept playing through her head. And the final scene, as Caroline was getting ready for bed, was of the two of them shopping in Tiffany's, selecting a big fat diamond ring!

On Tuesday, she did better at blocking the unwanted images from her mind. Fortunately, Mr. Hancock gave her a long to-do list. He was calling it the "just in case" list. All related to Evelyn's new packaging design. He wanted Caroline to get prices on the various materials required to manufacture the fancy satin chocolate boxes.

"Hopefully we won't need it." He crossed his fingers. "If we get lucky, Mr. Gordon will decide to wait until next year for this."

"I'll do my best to round up this information as well as the costs as quickly as possible," she promised. "Just in case." And then she'd spent the bulk of the day making phone calls, getting estimates, and making lots of notes.

On Wednesday morning, she felt she'd actually gotten the upper hand on her Technicolor mind-movie. In fact, she had nearly convinced herself that if Evelyn returned with a huge engagement ring on her finger, Caroline would simply take it in stride. She would warmly congratulate both of them and get on with her life. But when the phone rang just as she was getting ready to go to lunch, and she heard Mr. Gordon's voice, her previous resolve instantly melted.

"How are you doing, Mrs. Clark?" he asked with what seemed genuine interest.

"I'm fine," she told him. "Staying busy."

"And how's Joe? Still saving up for that baseball mitt?"

"Yes. As a matter of fact, he's actually working for my sister now, earning twenty-five cents a day."

"Enterprising young man. What does he do?"

"When he gets home from school, he's responsible for his young cousin Danny until suppertime. I'd say it's babysitting, but both boys take offense at that term."

Terrence laughed heartily.

"But I'm sure you didn't call long distance to hear about that." She put on her business tone. "How is New York?"

"New York is grand as always. Such a great old town."

"Did you lose the steak dinner bet?" As soon as it was out of her mouth, she regretted it. Why had she said that?

"Yes." He chuckled. "But I think it's a good bet to lose. In fact, that's exactly why I'm calling. Is your boss around?"

"He just stepped out for lunch," she said. "But he's probably in the break room. Want me to go look?"

"No, that's okay. I forgot that it would be lunchtime there. Why are you still at your desk?"

"I was just finishing up some things. I've been gathering estimates on the materials and whatnot for the new packaging. Just in case..."

"Good for you. And as it turns out, fortunate for everyone. Why don't you take a message for me, for Glen?"

"Okay." She picked up her pencil.

"Tell him we'll be going ahead. The new packaging idea has been a huge hit at the show. Pull out the stops and move forward. Bruce in Sales will call him later with some real numbers. But it's time to move. Not a moment too soon, either."

"Okay. Anything else?"

There was a brief pause. "No...I think that's all for now. Thanks for helping on this, Mrs. Clark. It looks like we've got a winner on our hands."

"That's wonderful."

"You have a good rest of your week," he said warmly. "I'll be back in the office on Monday."

"Travel safely," she said.

After she hung up, she grabbed her brown bag lunch and hurried to the break room, where she found Mr. Hancock sitting with Mr. Price. "I have good news," she said a bit hesitantly. "Well, I guess that depends on your perspective." She offered an uneasy smile. "Mr. Gordon just called. The satin heart design has been a big hit. He said to go forward with it, and he wants you to start production immediately. I put the full message on your desk, sir."

Mr. Hancock let out a little groan. "Okay...then I guess it's a done deal." He looked at Mr. Price. "You ready for this?"

Mr. Price rolled his eyes. "I just hope you package these things well enough to arrive at the stores looking as pretty as they did at the New York show."

"We'll do our best." Mr. Hancock turned back to Caroline. "Go ahead and start placing orders for the materials on the list. Hopefully we can start production the first of next week, if not sooner." He shook his head. "I better hire a few more employees."

For the next two days, Caroline spent most of her time getting the right materials lined up for the new satin packages. And, although her boss was less than enthusiastic, Caroline discovered that she enjoyed looking for the best materials for the best prices and the fastest deliveries. Mr. Hancock held several production meetings in his office, and instead of feeling like a mere secretary, Caroline almost felt as if she was a true part of the team. As they discussed the fabrics and ribbons and the way the construction of the boxes needed to happen, it seemed that they were actually listening to her ideas. And since she was the only woman—and perhaps more familiar with things like satin, lace, and velvet ribbons—they seemed eager to hear her thoughts.

By Monday, the materials were delivered, and on the following day, Caroline spent some time on the floor, along with the production managers, observing how the manufacturing process was actually going. "This is really interesting," she told Mr. Hancock as they watched a small team of workers assembling the specialty boxes.

"As you can see, the basic technology is the same as with our other boxes," he said. "But getting them to look like Evelyn's prototype isn't easy. Not without spending an inordinate amount of time—which equals money." He frowned at his clipboard. "If we can't start producing them about five times faster than we're doing right now, we will go into the red."

"Hopefully the workers will speed up as they get used to the process." She glanced at her watch. "I should probably get back to my desk."

He nodded grimly as he watched a worker fumbling to fasten a satin-covered button through the fabric and padding and into the cardboard part of the heart. "Thank you for all your hard work in getting us off to a fast start, Mrs. Clark."

As she returned to her department, she felt concerned for the new production crew. Assembling those boxes was a challenge! Fortunately, it wasn't her challenge. Caroline was relieved to get back to her desk. Due to the distraction these past few days, some of her daily chores had been neglected. It felt good to restore order and return to her routine. But as she sorted mail, she considered Mr. Hancock's concern over the expense of producing those fancy boxes. She hadn't really considered the cost of everything combined. The materials hadn't been cheap, and the workers' wages wouldn't be, either. She had no idea what the cost per box would be. Fortunately, that was Mr. Hancock's job. She just hoped it would all balance out eventually.

As the week passed, Caroline became painfully aware of two things. First of all, her boss was worried and distressed over the production of those "doggone" satin boxes. He'd already had one emergency meeting with Evelyn, hoping to convince her that it was necessary to simplify the design. However, she would not hear of it. The second thing troubling Caroline was that she had only seen Mr. Gordon twice. And both times he had been coolly professional and businesslike, treating her just like any other employee. While she knew that was probably for the best, she felt disappointed. And, although she tried to hide it, she felt blue.

Also, unless it was her imagination, many of her coworkers were feeling stressed and somewhat gloomy, too. It seemed everyone was on edge. Much of it was because they were in the midst of fulfilling Valentine orders and the pressure was high. But a lot of the tension seemed related to the fancy satin boxes—especially in her department. Sometimes it seemed that the only one with a positive attitude was Evelyn. Of course, Caroline realized that since it had been Evelyn's idea, she had to keep her spirits high. The only time Evelyn's perennial smile faded was when she ran into Caroline. And it all seemed to come to a head on Friday morning.

"*Excuse me*," Evelyn said in a disgruntled tone as she pushed past Caroline to reach the sugar container. "I happen to be in a hurry."

"I'm nearly done." Caroline dumped the spoonful of sugar in her boss's cup, moving out of the way so quickly that some coffee slopped out.

"And, in case you forgot, I happen to be a *vice president*," Evelyn snapped, reaching for the sugar. "In the first place, I shouldn't be getting my own coffee. In the second place, I shouldn't have to wait on *you*."

"I'm sorry." Caroline got a rag to wipe up the spilled coffee. "But I was getting Mr. Hancock's coffee. He's *also* a vice president."

Evelyn glared at her. "You seem rather uppity—for a *secretary*."

Caroline didn't know how to respond to this humiliation, but she was relieved they were the only ones in the break room.

"Maybe you think you can get away with disrespect," Evelyn continued, "because I'm a woman. Maybe you don't think I'm owed the same respect as a man in my position."

"I don't feel like that at all. I actually—"

"Or perhaps you resent me." Evelyn put her face close to Caroline's. "I am not blind."

"Blind?" Caroline cautiously backed away. For someone in a hurry, Evelyn certainly had a lot to say this morning.

"When it comes to Terry." She narrowed her eyes. "I know the score."

"I honestly don't understand what you—"

"I saw you at the New Year's Eve party. Cozying up to Terry's mother like you think she's your ticket to Terry. I know your type, Mrs. Clark. Opportunistic, manipulative— you take a job you don't really care about, playing the poor war widow, the helpless female in the workplace...but all you really want is to trap a rich husband."

"That's *not* true!" Caroline heard the break room door open and Evelyn's face immediately broke into a big smile.

"So, if you'll take my advice," Evelyn said pleasantly, "you'll discover that MG Chocolates is a *wonderful* place to work. You really are lucky to be part of the team, Mrs. Clark. Don't you think so, too, Terry?"

Caroline turned to see Mr. Gordon approaching the coffee area with a curious expression. "I guess so." He peered at Caroline. "Everything okay?"

"Of course." She held out the coffee cup. "Mr. Hancock's waiting for this."

It wasn't until she was in the production office that she realized she had tears running down her cheeks. How completely humiliating!

On Monday, a memo went out to the entire company. Caroline read it with only mild interest, knowing at once that she wouldn't participate.

Memo to All MG Employees & Golden Oaks Citizens.

Starting this week, the large front display window will
be transformed for Valentine's Day. Your Heart's Desire
is the theme, and everyone in the company and the entire town is invited to participate. Boxes of chocolates
can be purchased (with a hefty discount) and prominently displayed in the window, along with the name of
the recipient of the chocolates. But the catch is that the
giver of the chocolates will only be listed as "A Secret
Admirer." So start checking the window every day to see
if someone has left something there for you. Have fun!

Mr. Gordon

Just like that, everyone in the company—well, at least the
females—was all aflutter. Caroline tried to feign interest as
she sat with Doris and Mrs. Gallagher in the break room during the lunch hour, but the truth was she was still stinging
from Evelyn's attack on her the previous week.

"Mr. Price said Mr. Gordon only did this to lift everyone's
spirits," Doris was saying to Mrs. Gallagher.

"Yes, that's true," the older woman agreed. "But you must
admit it is a fun idea. I already called my husband to let him
know that I expect to find something in there." She laughed.

"I'm a little confused by it," Caroline admitted.

"How's that?" Mrs. Gallagher asked.

"It's just that I read in the employee manual that workplace
romance is grounds for termination. And I would think this
Valentine display might encourage romance between workers."

"You actually *read* the employee manual?" Doris asked.
"I've been here three years and I've never even opened it."

"Mr. Gordon *senior* put that old manual together quite some time ago." Mrs. Gallagher chuckled. "Mr. Gordon has pointed out that it needs updating."

"And there have been workplace romances," Doris pointed out. "No one got fired."

"Really?" Caroline felt slightly bamboozled now.

"And what about Miss Stuart and Mr. Gordon?" Doris asked.

"Well, no one knows for certain that it's an actual romance," Mrs. Gallagher reminded her. "To be fair, it's only a rumor."

"Whatever the case, I think the Heart's Desire window sounds like fun," Doris declared. "Even if I don't have a boyfriend." She laughed. "Maybe by Valentine's Day I will. Speaking of admirers, I hear that you have one, Caroline."

"What?" Caroline nearly choked on her bite of apple.

"A certain someone in Sales has expressed interest in you."

"But I—I don't even know anyone in Sales. Not really."

"Perhaps he's just admiring you from afar," Mrs. Gallagher suggested.

"Don't you even want to know who it is?" Doris asked enticingly.

"I don't really think so." Caroline glanced nervously around, hoping no one else was listening.

"Let's just say his initials are TS."

"Tom Stephens?" Mrs. Gallagher asked with interest.

Doris just nodded.

"Well, Tom is a very nice young man," Mrs. Gallagher told Caroline. "Hardworking and sincere. You could certainly do worse."

Caroline quickly gathered her lunch things. "Yes, I'm sure I could." And before they could make any more unwanted matchmaking comments, she excused herself.

By the end of the day, when Caroline was leaving the building, she noticed a group of women from the assembly line all gathered around the window. Already some boxes of chocolates were accumulating. And, just like the memo said, the names of the recipients were prominently displayed, but all the "from" lines only read: "Your Secret Admirer."

As Caroline walked past, she could hear the women giggling and speculating. And it seemed Mr. Gordon was right: They were having fun. Perhaps this would help to lift morale after all. Caroline knew that many employees, including her boss, were extremely stressed out. The specialty packaging seemed to become a bigger headache with each passing day. Not only was it costing too much to produce, it was taking too long. The goal had been to ship these expensive boxes with the last of the Valentine's chocolates this week so they'd be in stores and shops across the country just before Valentine's Day. From where they were standing now, it looked impossible. Unless her boss could get the other VPs to adhere to another plan. He had several in the works.

"Our only recourse might be to ship twice," Mr. Hancock had told Mr. Price this afternoon. The two men had this conversation in the waiting area by her desk.

"That'll cost more," Mr. Price warned.

"I *know* that." Mr. Hancock sounded terse. "But it might be our only hope."

"I'd like to hear what Finance thinks..."

"We better have a meeting." Mr. Hancock turned to Caroline. "It's too late to try to schedule it today, Mrs. Clark. But first thing in the morning, I want you to find a time when everyone can get together. I want an executive meeting before the end of the day."

She had promised to do so and even left herself a note, although she knew she wouldn't forget. As she walked home, she felt concerned for the sake of the company. Hopefully the VPs would be open to Production's ideas and solutions tomorrow.

Fortunately, the VPs couldn't meet until the end of the next day. That gave Caroline a chance to handle the chore list Mr. Hancock had given her, and it took most of the day to accomplish this. The meeting was scheduled for three thirty, and, like before, all the VPs and the secretaries took their seats. The only difference was that this time her boss was heading the meeting. And she had, according to his direction, brought a bag of samples with her—samples that she and a production crew had assembled earlier in the day. She'd also made sure that all the VPs had the short one-page agenda that Mr. Hancock had asked her to prepare this morning. Plus she'd asked Doris to help cover with note taking.

"As you can see by the agenda you received earlier today, we have a problem," he said solemnly. And now he went into the production challenges, explaining time constraints and budget concerns, the lack of assemblers, and finally pointing out the shipping dilemma, offering the option to schedule extra shipments.

"That's going to up our costs significantly," Mr. Price said.

"Just hire more assembly line people, work longer hours," Evelyn told him. "Get the packaging done sooner."

"We have a budget," Mr. Hancock reminded her.

"Well, we have to honor our accounts," Mr. Russell told him. "If we don't deliver the goods, we could lose them for future orders."

"I'm not saying we can't run a second delivery," Mr. Price explained, "but as you know that will double the cost."

"Or we could cut our losses and simplify the packaging,"

Mr. Hancock said finally. "Mrs. Clark, please present the new prototypes."

Caroline opened the bag and removed the first sample that their production team had designed. Unlike the one Evelyn wanted, this one wasn't padded and didn't have the cloth-covered buttons or the ruffled trim, but it was covered in satin and the velvet bow was in place. She laid it on the table and tried not to wince when Evelyn let out a loud groan of disappointment.

"That is ridiculous," Evelyn exclaimed. "It looks nothing like our prototype. The stores will laugh at us."

"That's just the first example," Mr. Hancock told her.

Caroline removed the second sample and began to understand her boss's thinking. This sample was just like the first one except that it had a lace ruffle.

"Humph." Evelyn just shook her head.

"It's not bad," Mr. Price said. "And it's not as if our accounts have photos or samples of the original prototype. It might work."

Mr. Hancock nodded to Caroline. "The third one."

Caroline reached into the bag. This one actually contained an idea that she'd suggested. Like the first two, it wasn't padded, but it did have the original ruffle and it also had one covered button that was centered into the velvet ribbon, which they had made into a larger bow.

"Now, that's not bad." Mr. Gordon came over to look more closely at the heart. "And honestly, if I didn't know better, I might think this was the same as what we took to the show."

"It's not nearly as nice," Evelyn said.

"But if we can't deliver on the original ones, we might have to compromise," he told her.

"I don't want to compromise," she said stubbornly.

"Do you want to risk everything just to have the original packaging?" he asked her.

"Why can't we just hire more workers?"

"Because of cost," Mr. Hancock said dryly.

"But we sold them with the prototype," she pointed out.

"We know that," Mr. Hancock said with surprising patience. "And now we know that the prototype is impractical. Do you really want to risk everything?"

She shrugged. "No, of course not."

"Okay," Mr. Gordon announced. "We'll go with the revised package. Will we be able to maintain our schedule and fulfill our orders, Glen?"

"Our chances just improved," Mr. Hancock said. "But it's still touch and go."

A little more discussion transpired before the meeting came to a close. Caroline quickly gathered the hearts and got out of the room along with the other secretaries.

"I think that new prototype is just as nice," Mrs. Gallagher told Caroline as they gathered around to look at it.

"I don't," Miss Thornton said sharply. "But I suppose it'll have to do."

As Caroline carried the packages back to the production department, she wondered why it seemed like both Evelyn and Miss Thornton still hated her. Was it simply because she'd gotten off on the wrong foot? Because she'd danced with Mr. Gordon at the New Year's Eve party? Would they ever get over it?

Chapter 14

As the week progressed, the Your Heart's Desire window steadily filled up. The boxes were smaller at first—mostly for assembly line employees—and then a few midsized ones appeared. By the end of the week, there were several larger ones, including one for Mrs. Gallagher, which everyone knew had been put there by her husband. But each day, before and after work, women would gather at the window, reading the tags and sometimes shouting an unexpected name out loud. Then they would make jokes about who the secret admirer might be, but it was clear they were enjoying it.

In fact, Caroline suspected she was the only one who wasn't enjoying it. "I feel like a spoilsport," she confessed to Marjorie during the weekend. They were sitting together in her sister's sparse living room, drinking coffee and watching as Lulu chased a ball back and forth across the floor. "I try to pretend to be interested, but the whole thing just makes me feel really sad and blue."

"That's too bad," Marjorie told her.

"I even saw your box in there," Caroline told her. "That was nice of Rich."

"What makes you think it's Rich?" Marjorie said in a teasing tone.

"I'll just be glad when Valentine's Day has come and gone," Caroline admitted. "I'm counting the days now."

"Is that because of your job?" Marjorie asked. "You really think the company won't offer you another position when Miss Bentley returns?"

"Mr. Hancock is predicting there'll be layoffs in every department," Caroline said glumly. "They'll start with the most recently hired employees," she said quickly. "Rich's job is secure."

"So that silly Valentine's package really messed things up?"

"Deliveries that should've been made this past week won't be going out until the end of next week. Less than two weeks before Valentine's Day. That's cutting it pretty close."

"Sounds like it."

"Anyway, I've already put in applications at some other businesses." Caroline took a sip of coffee. "No one's hiring that I know of, but I figured it wouldn't hurt." To change the subject, she brought up Joe's upcoming birthday. "If you don't mind, I'd like to have a little party for him."

"That's a great idea," Marjorie said.

"Just a few of his new friends," Caroline explained. "A cake and ice cream."

"I'll do anything I can to help."

"Thanks." Caroline knew she'd have her first paycheck right before Joe's birthday. And although she couldn't afford much and needed to be frugal since her next paycheck would be half

as large—not to mention her final one from MG Chocolates—
she wanted to make the party a good one.

By the end of January, the last of the Valentine's chocolates
were finally packaged and boxed and ready to be delivered, but
according to Mr. Hancock, their department's budget was in
bad shape. "I'll have to start laying off assembly line workers
by the end of the month," he told her in a confidential tone.

"Even with the Easter chocolate season ahead?" she asked.
"I've heard it's a busy time, too."

"Not busy enough to keep a crew this size," he said. "Not
this year."

Fortunately, the rest of the company seemed oblivious to
the problems ahead. Women were still clustering around the
Your Heart's Desire window. "Look, there's a new one," someone exclaimed as Caroline walked past on Friday morning.

"It's enormous!" someone else said.

"And it's for Miss Stuart," another said.

Caroline paused to see, and sure enough, there was an
enormous heart-shaped box with Miss Stuart's name on it.
Ironically, it was one of the original satin designs, the padded
one with covered buttons—and in the largest size.

"It's probably from Mr. Gordon," someone said quietly.
And everyone quickly agreed. Caroline turned away and
headed for the stairs. She'd quit using the elevator shortly after the day when Evelyn had torn into her in the break room.
It was the surest way to avoid running into Mr. Gordon or
Evelyn. Besides, it felt good to march up the stairs, as if she
was proclaiming her independence in doing so.

At lunchtime, Doris mentioned the oversized heart with
Miss Stuart's name on it. "Everyone is saying it's from Mr.
Gordon, but I'm not so sure," she told Caroline. "If you ask

me, whatever was going on between them has cooled down significantly."

"What do you mean?" Caroline asked with genuine curiosity.

"I mean I overheard them when I came out of the elevator a few days ago. It sounded like they were fighting."

"Maybe it was a lover's quarrel," Caroline tried.

"I don't think so."

"Then what about that big heart for Miss Stuart?"

"I think she put it there herself," Doris whispered. "It's probably empty."

Caroline laughed. It was the first good laugh she'd had in a couple of weeks.

"I'll bet I'm right," Doris insisted.

"How about the heart with your name on it?" Caroline teased. "I heard that Wally from the assembly line is responsible for it."

Doris grinned. "Wally's a nice guy, and not bad looking either."

They joked about it a bit more, but as Caroline returned to her office, she wondered. Was it possible that Evelyn and Mr. Gordon weren't as serious as Caroline had been trying to convince herself these past couple of weeks? Even so, Caroline didn't want to let herself think about it. She knew it was foolish to get her hopes up. Instead, she was determined to focus on work and the plans for Joe's birthday party this weekend.

As she left the building, the usual crowd was gathered at the window. "There's Mrs. Clark now," someone said. "Look, you've got a box of chocolates in there, too."

Caroline went over to see, peering at the spot where an assembly line woman was pointing. There, sure enough, it said TO CAROLINE CLARK FROM YOUR SECRET ADMIRER. Caroline stared at the box. It was larger than a midsized box, but not one of the overly large ones. Still, it was pretty with its red foil covering and lacy trim. In many ways, it seemed prettier than Miss Stuart's big pink padded box.

"Who do you think sent it?" Miss Warner the receptionist asked Caroline.

"I have absolutely no idea," Caroline confessed.

"A real secret admirer," Miss Warner proclaimed.

"I'll bet it's Jack Knowles," a woman said. "I heard that he likes Mrs. Clark."

"Or Mr. Stephens from the sales department," Miss Warner said in a knowing way. "He's had his eye on Mrs. Clark for some time."

Caroline just smiled, pulled on her gloves, and went outside. While it felt surprisingly nice to know that someone had purchased a box of chocolates for her, she wasn't sure she wanted to know who the secret admirer was. It didn't matter if he was from the assembly line or the sales department or even the moon; she knew she would have no interest in him. Still, it was sweet.

On her way home from work, she stopped by the bank to deposit her check, then went to the hardware store, where she purchased an airplane model that she knew Joe wanted, as well as a baseball. Then she went to a couple more stores, picking up various items for Joe's party: balloons, candy, and party favors, as well as a few baking ingredients. She knew it was a splurge, but it was fun, and they would have plenty of time to tighten their belts again next month.

Although she'd originally planned for this to be a surprise party, Joe had quickly figured it out. So even if he saw her making his cake tonight, it would be okay. Mostly he was looking forward to spending time with his friends, and he'd asked her if it was okay for them to go to the nearby park to play baseball after the party. She had been tempted to buy him the baseball mitt he so desperately wanted, but she knew he'd enjoy it more if he could purchase it himself. He'd worked so hard to save up for it. Plus she knew that the card her parents had sent this week would probably contain the extra cash needed to get it. She couldn't wait to see his eyes light up when he bought it.

On Saturday morning, she wished Joe a happy birthday and gave him his presents. He was delighted over the model plane and baseball. Then she presented him with the card from his grandparents, and just as she had guessed, they had tucked in two dollars. "Do you want to go to town and get that baseball mitt?" she asked him.

He looked down at the two bills, then shook his head. "Not right now," he said.

"Are you sure?" she asked. "I know you wanted to play ball with your friends today ... after the party."

"It's okay." He just shrugged. "I think I'll go upstairs and show Danny my presents. Okay, Mom?"

"Of course."

Due to the mild weather, they set up the party in the backyard. Marjorie put Lulu in the playpen as she helped Caroline. Together they made the picnic table look festive and fun, and before long Joe's four school friends arrived. Joe was the perfect host and even included Danny in the festivities and helped him to play the games that Marjorie had planned for all of them. Eventually it was naptime for Danny and Lulu. And the older boys gathered their bats and gloves and headed to the park to play ball.

"I can't figure why Joe didn't run to town and buy that baseball mitt earlier this morning," she told Marjorie as they carried things back into the kitchen. "I encouraged him to go, but he refused."

"Oh ..." Marjorie set the dirty dishes in the sink with an odd expression.

"I know he'd saved up nearly enough money," she continued. "It's been so generous of you to pay him for entertaining

Danny. And Mom and Dad sent him enough money to get it. And I can't imagine he'd have changed his mind."

"No...I wouldn't think so."

Caroline studied Marjorie. "It feels like you know something I don't know."

Marjorie gave her a perplexed expression.

"You do, don't you?"

Marjorie turned on the sink faucet.

"No." Caroline stepped in front of her. "I'm washing these things up. And if you're not going to spill the beans, I think you should go take a nap."

Marjorie chuckled. "You sound just like my big sister."

"What do you know?" Caroline demanded. "Why didn't Joe go get that mitt?"

"I'm not supposed to tell you." Marjorie's eyes lit up. "But if you could guess..."

"Guess?"

"Yes. Perhaps you've had some sort of surprise recently. Something you didn't expect."

Caroline thought hard. "The Your Heart's Desire window?"

Marjorie nodded. "He overheard us talking last week and he was worried about how sad you sounded."

"Oh, dear. Please don't say he sacrificed his mitt money for me."

"I actually tried to talk him out of it. I thought maybe I could sneak in there and get you a box of chocolates myself. But he insisted—it had to come from him."

"Oh, my." Caroline turned off the faucet and stared at Marjorie. "What a sweet boy, huh?"

Caroline nodded as a lump filled her throat, and suddenly both the sisters were crying and hugging each other. How had she ever managed to feel sorry for herself—with a son like Joe?

Chapter 15

It took Caroline a week to decide, but on Friday she knew what she needed to do. So during her lunch hour, she went to the hardware store to purchase the mitt that Joe had wanted so badly. She wasn't exactly sure how she would present it to him. Everything inside of her longed to give it to him tomorrow morning, so that he could take it to play baseball with his friends. But she was worried that might tip him off, and according to Marjorie, he had really wanted to keep it a secret. She didn't want to spoil it for him. She pondered her dilemma as she walked back to work. So much so that she didn't even notice Mr. Gordon standing by the entrance.

"You seem rather preoccupied." He held the door open for her.

"Oh?" She blinked in surprise, forcing a smile. "I suppose I was..." She paused by the Your Heart's Desire window and let out a small happy sigh to see Joe's heart still out there in front, shining like a bright beacon of hope.

"Looks like you have a secret admirer," he said as he stood beside her.

"Oh, yes," she cheerfully agreed. "I do."

"So I've heard."

"You've heard?" She peered curiously at him.

He knowingly smiled. "Oh, you know how people talk."

"Really? Are you suggesting that someone here knows who got me those chocolates?" she asked with a defiant expression. "I seriously doubt that."

"Don't be too sure." He walked with her toward the elevator, but when she just kept going toward the stairs, he followed. "I've noticed you've been avoiding the elevator lately. Worried about a mechanical failure?"

She laughed as she stepped onto the first step. "No, of course not." She continued going up.

"Why then?" he asked as he followed her up the first flight.

"Maybe I like the exercise," she said lightly. She paused at the second-floor landing. "Why are you taking them?"

"Maybe I like the exercise, too," he said in a teasing tone.

She stepped onto the next step, looking evenly at him from her vantage point. "So then tell me, what is it that people are saying about me? Who do they think put that box of chocolates in the window for me?"

He made a half shrug that reminded her of how Joe acted when he didn't care to answer a question. "You obviously know who put it there."

"Yes, I do know. But I'm curious as to this rumor you mentioned." She folded her arms across her front.

"Well, everyone seems fairly certain that Tom Stephens in Sales put it there." His expression became fairly serious. "But you obviously know that."

She laughed. "I know nothing of the sort. Although I do

know who my secret admirer is. He is in fact someone I'm terribly fond of. Someone I love dearly and would not want to live without."

Mr. Gordon looked slightly stunned. "Well...that's good." Now he turned around as if he was going back down the stairs.

"You don't want to know who it is?" She boldly reached for his arm, stopping him. "You seemed so interested."

He turned to look at her, and unless she was imagining it, there was hurt in his eyes. And suddenly she regretted this game she was playing. "It was my son, Joe," she declared. "The sweet boy used his baseball mitt money to buy it for me last week." Suddenly she felt those same maternal tears coming again. "It was supposed to be a secret, but I found out and..." She held up the package. "I just bought him this mitt and the reason I was so distracted just now was that I was trying to decide whether to give it to him tomorrow or wait until Valentine's Day."

And then, feeling very silly and emotional, she took off running up the stairs. She'd just reached the top of the fourth flight when she felt a hand on her shoulder.

"Wait," he said breathlessly. "I'm sorry. I shouldn't have treated you like that."

She turned to look into his eyes. "It's okay. I probably shouldn't have said what I did. It seems to have troubled you."

They stepped out of the stairwell, still looking at each other. "There's been a misunderstanding," he said, still catching his breath. "I've received misinformation from an unreliable source."

"Oh...?" She nodded. Somehow she felt like she knew which source he was referring to. Not that she cared to admit it to anyone. But, unless she was mistaken, she could hear the sound of the source's high-heeled shoes clipping down the hallway. "Evelyn?" The name escaped her lips almost without her knowing it.

"Yes," he said quietly. "That day in the break room, when you seemed upset and left quickly. I need to know—was Evelyn warning you to be careful about an office romance? An affair with Mr. Stephens?"

"No. Of course not." She firmly shook her head. "I've never said more than two words to Mr. Stephens. Evelyn was chastening me for not getting out of her way fast enough when she wanted her coffee. And for not respecting her position as a vice president. And then she was warning me about…well, something regarding you." The sound of the heels was getting closer.

"And is that why you seemed to have disappeared during these past few weeks?"

"Oh, there you are." Evelyn strode toward them. "I was just looking for you, Terry." She barely glanced at Caroline. "We need to talk. Now."

"Yes," he said firmly. "We do." Now he turned to Caroline. "If you will please excuse me, Mrs. Clark. Although I do hope to continue our conversation later. And I do have some thoughts on that mitt. In my opinion you should maintain the secret. Let him wait until Valentine's Day for it. And, by the way, since Joe's had his tenth birthday, he should start coming to Buckaroos. We meet after church. We will officially induct him this Sunday if he comes."

"Oh, thank you!" she said eagerly. And then, almost afraid this was all a good dream, she turned and hurried away. She couldn't explain why she felt so joyful, but it was as if she were floating as she went into the production department.

To Caroline's dismay, she didn't see Terrence for the rest of the day. As she slowly walked home, she wondered about their conversation on the stairs. She knew it had been real, but it still seemed rather strange and dreamlike. Unless she was imagining things, and she knew that was possible, it had almost seemed that he was about to declare his feelings for her.

But she knew that the whole company had been feeling a bit on edge all week, and even more so today. Another emergency meeting with the VPs had been called at the end of the day. "Mr. Gordon wants Mr. Hancock in his office by four o'clock. And tell Mr. Hancock the meeting will probably run late," Mrs. Gallagher explained. "And it's just the VPs and Mr. Gordon this time. The secretaries aren't required to be there."

Caroline suspected the meeting was related to the layoffs that were scheduled to take place next week. Somehow this information, like the romance rumors, had leaked into the gossip mill, too. And, naturally, job stability had taken precedence over the Heart's Desire window. Morale was steadily sinking.

When she got home, she tucked the baseball mitt package into her closet, but when Joe came down to greet her, she told him the good news about being inducted into the Buckaroos. "Mr. Gordon invited you himself," she assured him.

As Joe did a gleeful dance all over their apartment, she realized that the glove could wait a few days. As she fixed them dinner, she wondered what the conversation between Terrence and Evelyn had been like. As badly as she wanted to believe that Terrence had given Evelyn her walking papers, she suspected that hadn't happened. For one thing, Evelyn's family was close friends with Terrence's family. Besides that, Evelyn was actually really good at her job. But hopefully he had set her straight about a few things. Made it clear to her that he was the boss and what he would or wouldn't put up with. Mostly she felt glad that he knew . . . that he understood.

On Sunday morning, Caroline and Joe walked to church together. Wearing the periwinkle suit, she felt amazingly hopeful as she reached up to push a piece of windblown hair into place. She had arranged her hair in one of the looser styles that Marjorie said made her look chic and young. But after she and Joe parted ways, she suddenly felt nervous. Oh, she knew it was silly as she went into the sanctuary. After all, she was simply going to church. And even when she noticed that Terrence was sitting with his family and that Evelyn and her parents were sitting right next to him, she decided to pay it no mind.

Taking a seat in back, she told herself it was simply two families, ones that had been close for decades, sitting together. Nothing more. Instead of obsessing over it, she focused on the sermon and the beautiful light glowing through the windows, but as soon as church ended, her bravado faded as she slipped out of the sanctuary to find Joe.

"Are you ready for Buckaroos?" she asked him.

He nodded eagerly, looking over his shoulder to where a couple of boys were tearing down the stairs to the basement.

"Well, have fun," she told him. "Do you want me to come back here to walk you home later?"

He grinned. "No, Mom. I know my way back just fine."

She resisted the urge to run her fingers through his sandy curls. "Okay. See you later then." As she watched him hurrying toward the stairwell, she noticed Terrence and Evelyn at the other end of the hallway. They were chatting with another couple and a boy about Joe's age. Terrence had his back to her, but something he was saying was making the other couple laugh and smile. He was obviously putting them at ease.

There was something about that scene, maybe it was the way Evelyn placed her hand on Terrence's arm—in a way that seemed to suggest ownership. That, combined with just having seen the two of them and their families together in

church, well, it just unraveled what little confidence she'd recently gathered. And so, without saying a word to Terrence,
she found the nearest exit and headed for home.

As Caroline slowly walked through the sunshine, she reminded herself of how many times she had observed Terrence
interacting with others at work and other places. He always
showed everyone such kindness and generosity. It was simply
his way. Surely that was what he had been doing for her. Trying to make her feel a part of the team, helping her to adjust
to her new life here in California. Perhaps she had read him
all wrong. Certainly, it wouldn't be the first time.

On Monday, Caroline felt unsure about a lot of things as
she went into the chocolate factory. For one thing, she knew
that this was the week when Miss Bentley had informed everyone she planned to return to work. As far as Caroline knew,
it wouldn't be for a day or two. Still, it was unsettling. Especially since Caroline hadn't heard anything from any other
businesses in town. She also felt uneasy about the layoffs that
she knew were coming—primarily in her department, which
she felt some loyalties to. And, of course, the most disturbing
thing was trying to determine the status of her relationship
with Terrence. By now she almost felt like she'd imagined
the stairwell conversation. Or else she had misunderstood his
intentions. Maybe she should celebrate that her stint at MG
Chocolates was coming to a swift end. A few more weeks like
this and she might end up in the nuthouse!

She was barely through the front door when she heard the
twitters coming from the direction of the front display window. "There she is," Miss Warner said in an excited tone.
"Come here, Mrs. Clark, you have to see this." She grabbed
her by the hand, pulling her to the window, where a new, extremely large heart-shaped box was positioned on the very top

of the display. Almost as if it was playing King of the Hill. The handsome, shiny red box looked like a gigantic version of the one that Joe had gotten for her—and like his, her name was on it.

"Who could it be from?" a woman asked.

"Do you know?" Miss Warner asked Caroline.

Caroline just shrugged. "Sorry, I don't know."

"It's the biggest one by far," someone said.

"Someone must really like you," another added.

"I heard it's from Tom Stephens," a woman said.

And then, without sticking around to endure their questions and speculations, she hurried toward the stairs, but seeing the elevator open and no one inside, she decided to take that instead. As she rode up, she couldn't stop thinking about that enormous heart. *Could it possibly be?*

As she emerged from the elevator, she nearly ran smack into Evelyn. "Excuse me," she said as she stepped aside, bracing herself for a scolding for not being more careful—or a lecture on Evelyn's status.

"No, excuse me," Evelyn said in a polite but chilly tone. Miss Thornton was with her and both of them looked at Caroline with curious interest.

"Did you see your heart in the window?" Miss Thornton asked quietly.

Caroline just nodded.

"Impressive," Miss Thornton said as if she meant it.

"It must be from Tom Stephens." Evelyn stated this as if she knew it for a fact.

"Oh, really?"

"Yes. We assumed the other heart was from him," Miss Thornton confided, "but it seems we were wrong. I guess that was from someone else."

"Probably someone from the assembly line," Evelyn said with authority.

"Probably old Walt." Miss Thornton giggled. "I heard he fancies you."

"Anyway, I just wanted to tell you congratulations on snagging Tom. Based on the size of that candy box, he must be very interested. I'm guessing that boy won't be available much longer." Evelyn jabbed Miss Thornton with her elbow. "And there are some girls who weren't too happy to hear about that."

"Oh, brother." Miss Thornton rolled her eyes. "Is nothing sacred?"

"Anyway, I also wanted to say no hard feelings." Evelyn gave Caroline a catty smile. "So if I said something to offend you the other day ... well, my apologies." She laughed. "Once you get to know me, you'll realize that I tend to speak first and think later."

"One of your greatest charms," Miss Thornton teased.

"So, really, no hard feelings." Evelyn smoothed her platinum hair. "And good luck with Tom. Really, he's a nice guy. Good catch."

Caroline was too stunned to respond, and as she walked to her office, she wondered which of them belonged in the nuthouse now. But instead of trying to figure out that crazy conversation, she focused on getting Mr. Hancock his coffee and completing her morning chores.

It wasn't until lunchtime that she learned from Mrs. Gallagher that Mr. Gordon had made an emergency trip to a chocolate supplier in South America and wouldn't be back until Wednesday night. But, as far as Mrs. Gallagher knew, no one had been laid off yet. "I think the VPs decided to wait until after Valentine's Day," she said quietly.

"Valentine's Day is just three days away," Doris said. "I

can't wait to find out who's behind some of those Heart's Desire candy boxes."

"That will be fun," Mrs. Gallagher said.

"The engagement pool has been growing this week," Doris told them. "Rumor has it that Mr. G is going to propose to Miss Stuart when he gets back from his trip."

"That should be very romantic," Caroline said stiffly.

"Now tell us about Tom Stephens." Doris lowered her voice. "Is it true?"

"Is what true?"

"That he's going to pop the question? That you'll be engaged, too?"

"No, of course not." Caroline firmly shook her head. "I barely know the man. That's just another stupid rumor."

"That's what I told her." Mrs. Gallagher turned to Doris with a knowing smile. "Best not to listen to idle gossip, dear."

"But why would he get Caroline such a huge, impressive heart?" Doris asked.

"How do you know it's from him?" Mrs. Gallagher demanded.

"I heard it from a good source. Someone who saw him picking it out."

"Oh...?" Mrs. Gallagher's brow creased. "Well, I suppose time will tell."

Caroline didn't know what to think. Was it possible that Tom Stephens really was behind the mysterious heart? And if he was, what did she think about it? And, really, she didn't have time to worry about Tom Stephens right now. That was truly the least of her problems. Everyone knew that Miss Bentley's six-week recovery time ended this week. And that meant Caroline would soon be unemployed.

Chapter 16

The next two days passed uneventfully, except for a phone call Wednesday from Miss Bentley announcing that she planned to return to work Thursday, Valentine's Day. "But I do hope you'll stick around for the day," Miss Bentley cheerfully said. "I already spoke to Mr. Hancock and he felt it was a good idea. We can both work together, and you can fill me in on everything. That way you'll get to enjoy the Valentine's Day festivities before you leave."

Caroline reluctantly agreed, but as she walked home that evening, she felt certain she'd made a mistake. Perhaps she'd go into work in the morning, meet Miss Bentley, explain a few things, then say her goodbyes and go home. The last thing she wanted was to be forced to wear a cheerful smile as she "enjoyed the festivities," knowing that it was her last day on the job. Not only that, but these rumors about Tom Stephens were getting way out of hand. The idea of the attractive, mild-mannered man in Sales being her secret admirer was partially flattering, but mostly unsettling. How would she react if she discovered he was behind the Your Heart's Desire display? What would she say to him? If she took her sister's advice, she and Tom would be dating soon, planning a wedding by summer. But she did not feel ready for that. Not at all!

She found Joe in their apartment, working on the Valentines that he was expected to exchange with his classmates the following day. "Need any help?" she asked as she removed her hat.

"I'm almost done." He held up a card with a bear on it. "This one's for Jimmy. 'I can't bear to be without you.'" He chuckled. "Get it?"

"Yes." She made a forced smile. "Cute."

"Are you sad, Mom?"

"No," she said quickly. "I think I'm just tired."

"Did you figure out who your secret admirer is yet?" he asked with a twinkle in his blue eyes.

Now her smile turned genuine, remembering the sacrifice he'd made to get her the box of chocolates. "Not exactly. But I've sure had fun trying to figure it out. And I can't wait to open that box of chocolates. I hear they're a good selection."

"Yum!" He eagerly smacked his lips. "Do you get to have it tomorrow?"

"That's the plan." She hadn't told Joe about the other box—the gigantic one that everyone assumed was from Tom Stephens. So much was being said about it that she was almost starting to believe it herself.

"Is this your last week to work at the chocolate factory?" Joe's eyes darkened with concern.

"I'm afraid so."

"Are you worried, Mom?"

"I suppose I'm a little concerned." She unbuttoned her jacket. "But I've put my application in at a lot of places. And once I'm not working, I'll have time to go around town and talk to people. I'm sure that something will open up." She smiled. "Remember how I walked into MG Chocolates and got a job the same day?"

"Yeah." He nodded eagerly. "I bet that's what will happen again."

She ran her hand over his hair, looking at how neatly he was writing his classmates' names on the envelopes. "Those look very nice, Joe."

"Thanks. And I helped Danny do his Valentines already. He only has twelve kids in his class. I have twenty-two."

The next morning, Caroline put on the periwinkle suit as well as her "party" face. Determined to end her short stint at the chocolate factory with grace and style, she had decided to put in a full day's work—without a single complaint or frown for anyone. Not even Evelyn. As far as that business about Tom Stephens, well, she had decided to simply put it out of her mind. Or, like Scarlett O'Hara, she would think about it tomorrow.

Besides, she reminded herself as she carefully styled her hair in the way that Marjorie had taught her, she and Joe could use the extra money from a few extra hours of work. Who knew when another paycheck would come her way.

"I have a little Valentine's Day present for you." She held the baseball mitt behind her back as Joe emerged from the bathroom, with his hair all neatly combed into place.

"Really?" His brows arched. "I, uh, I have something for you, too. But I'll give it to you later...okay?"

She grinned. "Okay. Now guess which hand."

He pointed to the right one, and she held out the package. "Happy Valentine's Day, Joe."

As he peeled off the brown paper, he let out a happy

yelp. "Thanks, Mom! This is amazing! It's exactly the mitt I wanted! Thank you so much!" He hugged her tightly.

"You've been such a good sport about everything. The move here and helping with Danny." She leaned down and kissed his forehead. "Thanks!"

"I can't wait to show this to Jimmy." He eagerly grabbed his jacket. "Do you care if I leave early?"

"Not at all." She dangled the paper sack of Valentines. "Don't forget these."

She told him to have a good day and, still relishing the look of pure joy in his eyes, took her time walking to work. She planned to enjoy this day fully—the warmth of the sunshine on her back, the sounds of the birds flitting through the trees, the cheerful plants and flowers blooming along the way. California truly was a wonderful place, and despite knowing she would be jobless by the end of the day, she did not regret this move. Not one bit.

Caroline knew from what Mrs. Gallagher had said that Mr. Gordon would be back from his trip by now. She also knew that, as usual, a special catered luncheon would be served in the break room. And, unlike her experience with the New Year's Eve luncheon, she planned to partake and enjoy this one fully. Even if Evelyn showed up with a huge diamond ring and the "happy" news that she and Mr. G were engaged, Caroline would manage to keep her party face in place to the end of the day. Oh, she knew this was extremely unlikely, but somehow it comforted her to know that she could face the very worst if she had to. She just hoped that she didn't have to.

As she went into the building, she grew curious about the oversized heart with her name on it. Despite her resolve not to think about it, she knew she would have to face facts sometime today. What would she do if it really was from Tom

Stephens? How would she act when this was revealed? Already, due to her own embarrassment, she'd gone out of her way to avoid him of late. And, unless she was mistaken, he seemed to be avoiding her, too. Or else he was feeling shy. Whatever the case, it was probably a good thing this was her last day, since she had no idea how to handle this unsettling dilemma. Someone in this company really ought to read page nineteen in the employee manual.

As usual, the display case was surrounded by female workers, still twittering with speculations and expectations, pointing out a few boxes of candy that had been added since yesterday. Instead of ignoring the women, like usual, Caroline tossed out a friendly greeting, then headed for the elevator, where Doris was waiting with several others.

"I can't believe it's your last day," Doris said quietly as they rode up. "Are you okay?"

Caroline gave her a bright smile. "I'm perfectly fine. Thank you for asking."

But as soon as she went into the production department, she felt a wave of dismay. There, sitting at what had previously been her desk, was an attractive brunette. "You must be Mrs. Clark." She rose to shake hands. "I'm Miss Bentley."

"Welcome back." Caroline twisted the handle of her handbag, unsure what to do.

"Go ahead and put your things away," Miss Bentley instructed. "I already got Mr. Hancock his coffee. And he informed me there would be a company-wide meeting first thing this morning. Down on the production floor."

"Oh." Caroline went to the closet, finding a new spot for her things.

"I saw the display case downstairs. Looks like you've been having some fun around here." Miss Bentley winked. "That huge heart for you—I hear it's from Tom Stephens." She made a mock frown. "And a lot of the girls are furious. Including me. I've had my eye on Tom Stephens, too."

"I honestly don't think it's from him," Caroline explained. "We've barely exchanged words."

Miss Bentley waved a hand. "Oh, that's okay. I'm just glad that Mr. G isn't taken, too. Everyone keeps saying he and Miss Stuart will get engaged one of these days. I was worried it might've happened while I was gone." She laughed merrily.

Fortunately, it was time for the company meeting and Caroline was spared more of Miss Bentley's romance chatter. But as Caroline watched Mr. Gordon stepping onto a wooden crate, preparing to make some sort of speech, she felt a catch inside of her heart. And she knew that, in so many ways, she wasn't much different than Miss Bentley...or any of them. She was a romantic, too. And seeing Mr. Gordon just now filled her with some very mixed emotions.

Instead of giving in to these unsettling feelings, she kept a pleasant smile on her face, listening as he described his recent trip. "And I have good news for everyone," he said happily. "We have just landed a huge account. That's why I visited our cocoa suppliers, to make sure we can fulfill it." He went on to explain how well everything was working out and how the company needed to retain all the assembly line employees, and how everyone could celebrate that their jobs were secure. Well, everyone but her, Caroline thought glumly, as he finished his speech by reminding everyone of today's celebratory lunch. They all let out a loud cheer—including Caroline. Although her heart was not in it.

"Isn't that wonderful?" Miss Bentley said as they returned to the office. "I'd heard things were getting rough around here. A lot of folks expected to be out of work by the end of the week."

"Yes, it's very good news." Caroline forced a smile. "I'm so relieved for everyone."

She spent the next hour bringing Miss Bentley up to date on the state of the production office and explaining why she'd rearranged some of the files. "Of course, you can put it all back if you like."

"No, I think this makes sense." Miss Bentley paused to answer the phone. "Yes, Mrs. Gallagher, I'll let her know right now. Thank you." She hung up the phone and turned to Caroline. "You're wanted in Mr. Gordon's office. Sounds like it's related to the termination of your job." She made a sympathetic face. "Sorry."

"Oh, well." Caroline made a half shrug. "I better go then." As she walked around the catwalk toward the president's offices, she felt a tiny glimmer of hope. It didn't make sense that Mr. Gordon would call her to his office to terminate her job. That would be up to Mr. Stokes. Perhaps Mr. Gordon planned to offer her another position. And in light of this morning's speech, it seemed reasonable.

Mrs. Gallagher greeted her warmly. "Go right in. He's expecting you."

"Good morning, Mrs. Clark." Mr. Gordon stood as she entered his large and handsomely decorated office. She returned his greeting, giving him a pleasant smile as she attempted to ignore the fluttery feeling inside of her chest. "Please, have a seat."

"Thank you." She sat down, smoothing her skirt with her hands. "Congratulations on the new account. That was wonderful news for everyone."

His face lit up. "It's a *huge* relief. The last thing I wanted to do was to let people go." Now he got more serious. "Which brings me to your situation, Mrs. Clark. I hear that Miss Bentley has returned and this is your last day."

She nodded. "That's right. But I've really enjoyed my time here."

"There's a rumor going around, Mrs. Clark, about you and Tom Stephens." His dark eyes twinkled with what seemed mischief.

"But I already told you that wasn't true," she said a bit defensively.

"I'm not talking about the box of chocolates from your son. I'm talking about the huge heart-shaped box." He tapped his fingers on the desktop, watching her. "You're certain *that's* not from Tom?"

"I guess I can't be certain. But I have no reason—well, aside from gossip—to believe that it is."

"Do you know who it's from?"

She felt a fluttering in her heart as she shook her head. "No..."

"It must be from someone who's very interested in you..."

She felt a warm surge go through her. "It would seem so."

"And you're not the least bit curious as to who it might be?"

"Of course I'm curious." She sat up straighter. "And that brings me to something that's been bothering me lately, Mr. Gordon, something I read in the employee manual. In fact, I was instructed to read it specifically."

"What's that?"

"Page nineteen. It says that romance in the workplace is grounds for immediate termination. I don't understand how you can encourage that Heart's Desire display case without contradicting the rules in the manual."

"That's just what Mrs. Gallagher was telling me." He chuckled. "And you make a good point." His face grew serious. "For that reason, I am forced to terminate you, Mrs. Clark."

"What?" She frowned, then slowly shook her head. "Well, I guess it doesn't matter since my job ends today anyway." She started to stand.

"Wait a minute." He held up his hands. "We're not done here."

She sat back down and, feeling confused, she waited. "Yes?"

"Did you give Joe his baseball mitt yet?"

Feeling even more confused, she simply nodded. "Yes. For Valentine's Day. He was thrilled."

"I'll bet." He leaned forward. "Now, tell me, who do you think sent you the big Valentine's heart?"

"Well, for sure, it's not from Joe. He could never afford it. And I honestly have no reason to think it's from Tom Stephens. If you ask me, he's been framed." She studied him closely. He was clearly enjoying this. So much so that she wondered . . . was it possible . . . ? "Who do *you* think sent it?" she asked pointedly.

He laughed. "You really don't know, do you?"

She shook her head no, but her heart was feeling hopeful . . . *could it be from him?* Dare she hope that it was? And then, even if it was, did she really want to continue this roller-coaster ride of a relationship? One day she'd be blissfully happy, and the next day she'd find out he was engaged to Evelyn. No, she did not need this kind of drama and emotion.

He stood up and walked over to sit in the chair next to her. "Of course, it's from me. I really thought you knew that, Caroline." He smiled. "May I call you Caroline?"

She blinked, then nodded. "Sure . . ."

"And you must stop calling me Mr. Gordon. Please, call me Terrence."

"Okay . . . *Terrence.*" She loved how it sounded coming out of her mouth.

"Caroline, you turned my head that first day we met in the coffee shop. I was smitten by the gorgeous girl in the pretty dress, a cashmere sweater draped over your shoulders. I looked into your eyes and that was it."

"Really?" She was almost afraid to breathe. Was this a dream?

"And New Year's Eve, in your beautiful red gown, when you nearly beat me at pool. Well, I was gone for good by then." He took her hand in his. "But you're right about workplace romances—they do cause problems. And for that reason, I can't offer you another job here." He grinned. "But I'd like the chance to offer you something else."

"What's that?" Her heart was pounding hopefully.

"For starters, I'd like to invite you to dinner tonight. I mean as my date. And, as you know, that could be problematic if you were still employed here."

She slowly nodded. "Yes, that could be troublesome."

"So what do you say—will you be my date for Valentine's Day?"

"Yes—of course. I'd love to be your date."

"And if I'm lucky, this will simply be the first of many more dates." His eyes twinkled happily.

"I hope so." She smiled shyly. "Happy Valentine's Day, Terrence."

"Oh, it is a happy day." He reached for her hand and pulled her to her feet. "Consider yourself unemployed as of now, Caroline Clark." And then he took her into his arms and kissed her. "Happy Valentine's Day, dear!"

The Rest of the Sweet Story

As it turned out, Terrence had been right. Their memorable date on Valentine's Day was simply the first of many. And Terrence did not hold back on adventurous dates, including several hair-raising airplane flights that both Joe and Caroline loved, and he threw in some boat trips and beach picnics and anything else that was unexpected and spontaneous and fun.

A few people in town—and in the chocolate factory—called it a whirlwind romance, but Terrence's mother claimed she saw it coming on that first evening she'd met Caroline. "It was just a matter of time," Gladdie bragged to her friends later that spring.

Caroline grew accustomed to the occasional bouquets of flowers at her new job or generous boxes of chocolates during their courtship, but when Terrence presented her with an enormous heart-shaped box of chocolates on the Fourth of July, she was puzzled.

"Were these left over from Valentine's Day?" she asked cautiously.

Terrence laughed. "I assure you they are fresh. Come on, open it up. Try one."

So she carefully removed the lid, and as the sweet aroma of chocolate wafted up, she noticed something bright and sparkling in the center of the box. Blinking in surprise, she reached for what had to be a piece of costume jewelry. "Is this some new marketing gimmick for next year's Valentine's chocolates?" She stared at the gorgeous ring—a heart-shaped diamond surrounded by lots of small bright rubies.

He chuckled. "That'd be one mighty expensive Valentine's Day campaign."

She picked up the ring, feeling its weight, and knowing that it was for real. "What's going on here, Terrence?" But when she looked up, she realized that Terrence was down on one knee—a very serious expression on his face.

"Will you make me the happiest man on earth by agreeing to become my wife?" he tenderly asked. "I love you, Caroline, and I promise to do everything I can to make you the happiest woman on earth."

"You already have," she said as they embraced and kissed. "Yes, I will gladly marry you!"

News of their engagement spread like wildfire. Some seemed shocked, but most, including Doris and Mrs. Gallagher, claimed they saw it coming. Evelyn acted completely nonchalant—and as if their engagement had nothing to do with the marketing job she accepted in New York City a few days later. Marjorie and Rich couldn't have been happier for her, although Marjorie begged her not to schedule the blessed event until Lulu was old enough to be the flower girl. And

Caroline's parents were over the moon at the good news, hastening the moving date to join their family in California.

Young Joe had been Caroline's biggest concern, but she quickly discovered that her worry was for nothing. Gaining a new dad who flew an airplane, liked playing ball, and was also the fearless leader of the Buckaroos was a win-win-win for him.

It was on Valentine's Day of 1947, in the presence of family and friends, that the couple repeated their marriage vows in the crowded church with the sun shining through the beautiful stained-glass windows. Joe stood up as Terrence's best man, and Marjorie was Caroline's matron of honor.

And Mr. and Mrs. Gordon continued celebrating that romantic anniversary date for nearly six decades—with three children, and seven grandchildren, and nine great-grandchildren...to carry on the tradition and sweet memories for them.

If you enjoyed *Your Heart's Desire*, look for these
Valentine's Day novels by Melody Carlson

Once Upon a Winter's Heart

Emma Burcelli concludes that love is officially dead when her grand-
father, Poppi, suddenly passes, leaving her grandmother, Nona, devastated. To help out, Emma works in the family bookstore. Although
she feels like a V-Day Scrooge, Emma quickly learns to enjoy the task
of decorating the store for Valentine's Day with the help of a handsome family friend, Lane Forester. As Emma and Lane share time and
memories of Poppi, she reconsiders the notion that romance is *alive*.

Just as Emma's heart begins to lift, however, she learns her sister
has already staked a claim on Lane. Emma's mother and sister insist
that Lane sees her only as a future sister-in-law, but she can't help
wondering if it could be something more.

Love Gently Falling

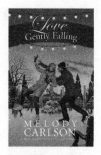

Rita Jansen is living her dream as a hairstylist in Hollywood when her father calls with news that her mother has suffered a stroke. When she gets home to Chicago, Rita finds her mother is healing but facing a long recovery. Worse, without being able to run their family-owned salon, her mother could lose the business. Rita decides to help, but she only has until Valentine's Day to come up with a plan.

As Rita takes her mother's place at work, the nearby skating rink she loved as a child brings back fond memories. Rita also finds herself renewing friendships with her childhood best friend, Marley, as well as her classmate Johnny. Although they now lead such seemingly different lives, Rita is surprised by how well she and Johnny connect and how far he will go to help her. Though Rita believes Johnny is only being kind, with romance kindling in the air and on the ice, their friendship may just fall into something more.

CENTER STREET

Available now in print and electronic formats from Center Street wherever books are sold.